I0700169

Of Poison and Passion

A Vexia Novella

Mallory Wanless

Content warning

Of Poison and Passion is a New Adult Fantasy Romance. There are some flashback scenes of sexual abuse, violence against children, mild blood and gore, and hints at spousal abuse. If any of these things might upset or trigger you, please don't read this book. Not all books are for all readers. I don't want anyone to be hurt by my words.

Dedication

To Buffy, my sourdough starter that just won't die.
I love you. You made me a confident baker and I'm eternally
grateful.

Chapter 1

"Have you ever considered not killing people?"

"You know I have! But come *on*, this kind of money could set us up for the rest of our lives."

"There's bound to be an easier way for you to make coin. Paid assassin just sounds so dirty."

Leah rolled her eyes dramatically. "Gods, Tameer. You can't be serious. That's the pot calling the kettle, isn't it? From the head of the Thieves Guild, no less. Besides, it was never just about the money. I enjoy my work. Do you know how hard it is to create new, never-before-seen poisons? It takes years! Not to mention all the time I've devoted to building up my own natural immunity to these same poisons. This is no easy feat, pal. I've dedicated my life to my craft. I'm a perfectionist."

She sat back proudly, grinning from ear to ear at the look of annoyance on her best friend's face.

Tameer had been her confidant and trusted friend for over a decade, and considering she was only twenty-three, that was really saying something. They'd come up in the same street gang together, picking pockets and swiping food from vendors' stands. One played lookout or distraction while the other stole what was needed. It was only in recent years that their paths had begun to split.

Tameer had taken over the Thieves Guild when Shithead—that was the name he'd given himself, clearly not a genius—had been taken out by rivals.

Well, that was the well-known story, anyway. In truth, Shithead had been Leah's first kill. He'd been in the middle of one of his "training sessions" with one of the new recruits—a girl who couldn't have been more than ten—when Leah had found him. She hadn't hesitated, driving her makeshift blade into the back of his head, right at the base of his skull. It had been pure luck that he'd died instantly. Better than the bastard deserved.

Leah had taken the girl across the bridge, into the nicer part of Ravendale, and left her on the front steps of the Mothers of Mercy temple. The religious sect was obnoxious, but they had a good reputation. Leah had intended to escape there long ago, but they wouldn't allow men, even boys, and she refused to leave Tameer alone.

When she'd returned to dispose of Shithead's body, Tameer had been waiting. He'd seen what she'd done. She'd been afraid that he would judge her, hate her, or even worse, be afraid of her. To her shock and relief, he immediately pulled her into a tight embrace, stroking her hair and whispering kind things into her ear. That was the last time she allowed herself tears.

Once her tears had dried up, she and Tameer had thrown Shithead into the river and returned to the guild's hideout. They agreed that Shithead had too many loyal members of the guild to tell them the truth; Leah didn't want to get killed in retribution. Instead, they concocted a story. The guild's biggest rival had been making a lot of noise lately, picking fights and causing trouble. They decided to tell the guild that Shithead had been taken out by their rivals and his body had been thrown away.

Leah hadn't been sure it would work, but Tameer had a way with people. He spoke and they always listened. The next day, their guild was in a full-fledged war with their rivals.

By the end of the week, their rivals were no more.

"But this time it's a king. You've never been hired for something this big before." Tameer was nervous, understandably, but his fears were misplaced.

"He's not *my* king."

"Only because you refuse to acknowledge any authority other than your own." Tameer huffed irritatedly.

Leah raised her arms out confidently. "And look how well that's worked out for me!"

Tameer rubbed his temples, releasing a frustrated breath. "You're going to get us both killed one day."

Leah took his hands in hers, beaming up at him with her classic overconfident grin. "Nah, we'll be fine. I'm unkillable."

Famous last words.

The tavern was crowded and smelled like piss and stale beer. Ash didn't want to be there any longer than was absolutely necessary. His intel had alerted him to the fact that an assassin had been hired to take out the king. As captain of the King's Guard, Ash took personal offense to this. The king might have been a self-serving, violence-prone monster, but he was still the king. Ash wouldn't allow him to be murdered by some hired assassin.

His spies hadn't had much information about the assassin; the murderer was something akin to a ghost. No one knew what they looked like, or even their gender. It was going to make finding them challenging, but Ash never backed down from a fight.

He stepped up to the bar, looking as inconspicuous as possible. Keeping a watchful eye on the room, he nodded to the barkeep. Geoffree was a good man, for a retired criminal. He'd hung up his lock picks long before Ash became captain, but the man was still hard-wired into Mistfall's countrywide criminal network. Geoffree wasn't an informant, but he would occasionally slip Ash information if he thought the crime in question might harm his bottom line. Harboring a would-be treasonous assassin would definitely cause Geoffree some issues.

"What canna get ye, Cap?" Geoffree asked around the cigar dangling from his fat lips.

"Information." Ash took a seat at the bar, keeping his back to Geoffree as he surveyed the room.

"Well, we've got a couple hookers in tonight, if you're looking for some company. I hear one of them is even clean." Geoffree slammed a tankard of flat, warm ale on the bar behind Ash.

"Not the information I'm looking for," Ash replied flatly.

Geoffree chuckled once more, then nodded to a table in the far corner of the crowded bar. Two creatures sat there, huddled close as they carried on some private conspiracy.

The shorter of the two creatures seemed to have pink hair, but that was more likely a trick of the light. Only fae had hair like that, and there hadn't been a fae in Ravendale in decades. King Odker had been quite systematic about removing them from the capital and surrounding towns when Ash had still been a babe on his mother's tit. He heard stories, growing up, about the fae. Their magic. Their skill with stealth and plants. It was no small wonder that they all became assassins and murderers.

Recognizing the girl for what she was, Ash knew she must have been the one who'd been hired to assassinate the king. He gave Geoffree a quick nod of thanks and slipped into the crowd, making his way toward the would-be murderess and her companion. If he was lucky, he'd be able to overhear their plans, ensure nothing had been set into motion already, and take out the pink-haired villain before sunrise.

Chapter 2

Leah and Tameer were regulars in the town's only tavern, which made it painfully obvious when the stranger entered the bar. He wasn't a local, of that she was sure, but he seemed friendly enough with Geoffree that Leah felt sure he wasn't a threat. At least, not at first. She'd seen him in the tavern a few times in the last couple of years, but tonight was different. The stranger had an air of coiled tension in his movements. His eyes surveyed the room as though he were a hunter seeking his prey. It was sexy, if a little unsettling.

Leah watched him through her lashes, keeping up her conversation with Tameer while giving most of her attention to the stranger. He was tall, at least a head taller than her. His arms were banded with ropes of hard muscle and thick veins. From her vantage point, it looked as though he might have a scar across his neck, but it had to be a trick of the light. Someone with a scar like that... would have had to survive an attempt at slitting their throat.

Tameer was saying something about their bread orders for tomorrow as Geoffree placed a tankard of ale behind the stranger and pointed him in the direction of the newest hookers in town. Leah nearly laughed out loud at the look of disgust that crossed the stranger's face. So high and mighty. He looked down his nose at those who use their talents to improve their lives. Clearly, he'd never wanted for a meal in his life. That much was evident by the muscle mass on his frame as well as his haughty demeanor.

"Are you even listening to me?" Tameer's annoyed voice cut through her thoughts.

Without taking her eyes off the stranger, Leah repeated back everything Tameer had just said. "We've got an order for three loaves of sourdough, a dozen lavender cookies, and upside-down cupcakes being picked up at noon tomorrow. I heard you, I'm just watching this creeper. He's been staring at us for the last two minutes and now he's moving closer."

Tameer shifted in his seat, subtly, angling his head to seem like he was leaning closer to talk to her, but in reality, she knew he was getting a better vantage point with which to see their stalker. Throwing his arm around her, Tameer gave the outward appearance of a man thoroughly smitten and hopeful for a night of pleasure. In truth, it was a show they'd put on many times in Ravendale when she'd needed him to help with her cover as she tracked a target.

Leah leaned into him, throwing her head back and tossing her curly pink hair over her shoulder as she pressed her face into Tameer's neck.

"Do you see the way he's stalking us?" she whispered into her best friend's skin.

Tameer nodded, slipping his fingers into her hair and appearing thoroughly engulfed in her affections.

"He moves like a soldier, not an assassin."

Tilting her head, Tameer brushed his lips against the shell of her ear. "He's fixated on your hair. He's got a dagger in his boot, but no other visible weapons. How do you want to play this?"

Leah sighed into him, wrapping her arms around his neck and practically climbing into his lap. "I don't want to risk a tavern brawl. Let's get out of here and see if he follows. Toss an extra coin to Geoffree on the way out. He'll know to have a couple of the miller's boys catch our stalker if he tries to follow us."

This was a backup plan she'd had with Geoffree and the miller's boys for the past few months. She'd put it into place when it seemed as though the hitters had stopped coming for Tameer. Couldn't be too careful. Leah liked to relax and enjoy her time at the tavern, but that didn't mean she was ready to leave Tameer completely unguarded.

Tameer stood from his chair, lifting her with him and wrapping her legs around his waist. Gripping her ass firmly, he strode to the bar, tossing the extra coin and triggering their fail-safe. Geoffree took the coin and gave Leah a knowing wink.

To the outsider, it looked as though she and Tameer were so infatuated with each other that they couldn't be bothered to have an inch of space between them. Leah's fingers gripped the short hairs at the base of Tameer's head, making a show of planting open-mouth kisses on his neck and nibbling his ear lobes. Tameer growled at her actions. In any other situation, the sound would have sent the message of eager arousal, but Leah knew he was anything but aroused by her actions. To show his appreciation for what he would later claim was "defiling his body with her filthy tongue", he swatted her ass. Hard. An unexpected yelp escaped her lips.

"Watch it," she growled into his ear.

"You started it."

Geoffree laughed at their antics as Tameer strode out the door and into the night.

Over his shoulder, Leah saw their stalker move to follow, only to be blocked by a sudden fight breaking out between the three barrel-chested brothers. Thank the gods for the miller and her boys.

Locking the door behind her, Leah peeked out the window in their kitchen, making sure they hadn't been followed.

"You know he's here for you." Tameer dramatically wiped his neck and ear where her lips had been just moments ago.

"That's offensive," Leah scoffed.

"You accepted a job to kill the king, and then a member of the King's Guard shows up? Be as offended as you like, but he's definitely here for you."

"Not that. You're right, he's here to stop the assassination. It's cute that he thinks he can. I'm offended by your behavior toward my affections. Most guys would kill to have my lips on their skin." Leah tossed an exaggerated wink at her best friend.

"Not all guys like girls, Leah. It's that simple. Not to mention, you're like a sister to me. I have *never* been attracted to you."

"Wow, you really know how to boost a girl's ego, Tam." Leah rolled her eyes. She wasn't attracted to him either, but he could at least try to hide his disgust for a minute. Shit.

"What are we going to do?" Tameer asked, peeking out the window again.

"Right now, we're going to feed Buffy and get some sleep. We've got a lot of orders in the morning, remember?" Leah opened the cabinet beside the stove and pulled out the jar containing her sourdough starter. Retrieving the bag of flour she'd bought from the miller that morning, she fed the starter—Buffy, the unkillable—and covered her back up, returning her to her spot in the cabinet.

"You're just going to bed? With a soldier clearly on the hunt for you?" Tameer stared at her, truly struggling to comprehend her actions.

"Yeah. I'm not going to go out and kill him right now, so I might as well get some sleep and prepare for our day tomorrow. This is my town, not his. I will not let some arrogant soldier in that asshole of a king's private guard mess with me in *my town*. I'll set some extra traps around all the doors and windows, but we need to get some rest. Lots to bake tomorrow!"

Ash watched from the shadows of the trees surrounding their home. The little assassin and her friend put on a good show but he knew better than to take the actions of a fae at face value. Once he'd gotten passed the drunken brawl, he'd slipped into the shadows and followed them back to their cottage.

At first glance, it looked like any other home in the small village. Upon closer inspection, however, Ash could see a handful of traps encompassing the property. He couldn't reach the house without triggering at least one of them, which meant she likely had the entire house locked and loaded. A spider wouldn't be able to enter that house undetected. He'd have to find another way to get to her. Ash refused to let that little fae kill the king.

That was his job.

Chapter 3

Being the only fae in a one-hundred-mile radius was a challenge, but not one that Leah shrank from. When she'd first come to Ravendale as a child, she'd been offended and enraged by the off-hand comments people made about her, assuming she was some sort of violent creature simply because she wasn't human. Then she learned that it wasn't because she wasn't a boring human. No, they assumed she was a murderer because she was fae. Her pink hair was the only indication of her non-human status, but it was enough to condemn her.

Leah's mother had been raped which resulted in her birth. Her mother hadn't even known her rapist had been fae until Leah's hair started to grow in when she was about a year old. Supposedly, fae were born bald in an effort to keep the babes safe. Or just because curly hair takes *ages* to grow in. Either way, her mother, who hadn't been thrilled by Leah's existence in the first place, had been devastated to learn that the child she'd borne by her rapist was fae. According to the nuns at the orphanage, that was why her mother had abandoned her on their doorstep. It's safe to say, these "bedtime stories" by her religious caretakers were one of the deciding factors when Leah chose to pack up and run away at only eight years old.

Tameer was the one who saved her from a group of belligerent drunks who thought they'd win the king's favor by bringing him the head of a fae. Tameer, who was eight at the time as well, convinced the men that he would guard her while they had one more celebratory drink before carrying her off to the king. The second the men had turned their backs, he grabbed her hand and took off running, weaving between dark alleyways and disappearing with her into the night.

The next day, he'd helped her dye her hair with ash and mud, disguising the rose gold hue of her curly locks and helping her hide in plain sight.

Over time, their relationship grew more mutually beneficial. As Leah spent more time on the streets, she began to hone her fae skills, quickly becoming one of the most efficient pickpockets in the capital. By the time her body flourished into a curvy female form, she'd become an expert at misdirection, seduction, and all manner of thievery.

Shithead might have been her first kill, but her first paid assassination was a guard who'd been taking advantage of the ladies who worked the corners at night. One of the girls had just found her friend, broken and bloody, half-hidden in a dark alleyway. In a rage, she grabbed Leah by the collar of her threadbare tunic and offered her ten coins for the man's head. Twenty for his cock.

Leah made thirty coins that night. More than she'd ever had in her entire life.

Her efficiency with a blade drew the attention of the assassin's guild, and she was quickly assigned to train under one of their more aggressive members. Unfortunately, her mentor was more interested in her body than in improving her skill set. After a week of his uninvited visits to her bed—well, her pallet on the floor of the cellar—she wet her blade with his blood. She hadn't killed him, but she hadn't intended to.

He went to the guild, demanding their approval so he could kill her—killing a fellow guild member without their express permission was suicide—but to Leah's amazement, the guild laughed in his face. The guild leader, Natalia, was a vicious woman who didn't tolerate ineptitude. Learning that he'd lost his manhood to a girl twenty years his junior had amused her and resulted in his swift death.

Natalia then took Leah under her wing, commending her for her poetic punishment of her previous mentor and ensuring that no other man in the guild felt they had a right to any female's body.

Leah spent years training with Natalia and quickly became the guild's most sought-after assassin.

Nearly a year ago, when Leah had decided to leave the capital and seek out a quieter life in Vexia, a small town on the outskirts of Ravendale, Natalia had tried to convince her to stay, even offering to double her pay. Leah appreciated the woman's efforts to keep her around, after all, who wouldn't enjoy feeling wanted and desired? But she had grown tired of the daily grind. Being the most sought-after also meant Leah had created a lot of enemies. Loved ones of those she'd killed, less skilled assassins who wanted her job, those who thought they were better than her simply because of her fae parentage.

Leah left Ravendale without looking back, taking Tameer with her as he had run afoul with his guild and needed a respite from their vengeance.

Tameer refused to tell her exactly what went down between him and his guild, but he made it clear that they no longer respected his authority and he needed a place to lay low for a while.

They settled in Vexia after a week of aimless travel. In reality, they hadn't ventured that far from Ravendale, and anyone who wanted to find them, could easily. However, after Leah killed the third would-be assassin sent after her friend and maimed the fourth, she sent them back with an unequivocal message: Tameer is protected and anyone who comes for him will regret it, assuming they lived to tell the tale.

Leah used a chunk of her coin to buy a small house in the middle of the woods and she and Tameer relaxed into a relatively peaceful life. After six months in their new home, her garden was thriving—some crops for their meals, but mostly poisonous plants. She might have retired, but she wasn't about to quit her passion projects.

Tameer struggled at first. He'd been the leader of the Thieves Guild for years. Going from boss to unemployed housemate had been a big adjustment for him. Leah recalled, rather vividly, the night they finally had it out.

She'd come home from selling their excess potatoes in the town market to find him in his cups, slumped over the dining room table. Leah had lost it. Using the ewer from their rain barrel, she dumped the icy water on his head, soaking his clothes and sobering him up *really* quickly.

"What the hells, Leah?!" He had the nerve to look annoyed and indignant.

"What the hells is right, Tameer. What the hells are *you* doing passed out, drunk off your ass? Gods, the sun has barely set and you can hardly stand." Leah stormed to the stove, loudly slamming the kettle on the burner and stoking the flames. "I get that you're unhappy, but this was your choice. I didn't kidnap you and make you come with me. I would have been fine on my own here, but now I'm forced to babysit your drunk ass every night."

Tameer grumbled something under his breath but didn't risk voicing it loud enough for her to hear him. At least he wasn't a complete idiot.

"I don't know what I'm doing here, Leah." He brushed wet hair from his face as he closed his eyes and exhaled in defeat. "Maybe I should have just stayed in Ravendale."

Leah turned, leaning back against the kitchen counter as she waited for the water to boil. "If you'd stayed, you'd probably be dead by now. I don't know who you pissed off, but damn, Tam, they were coming for you *hard*."

"I slept with someone I shouldn't have." His words were quiet, a hint of embarrassment in his voice. Not remorse though, that was interesting.

"You must've been pretty bad at it, if they kept sending assassins after you," Leah teased.

Tameer glared at her through his lashes. "You know I've never had any complaints before." It was true, Tameer might have been the leader of the Thieves Guild, but his forte remained solidly in the art of pleasure.

Their conversation stalled as the kettle began to sing. Leah made two cups of strong tea, placing a steaming mug before her friend as she joined him at the table. "What the hells is going on, Tam?"

Tameer didn't say anything for a long time. Leah was about to give up and start dinner when he finally spoke.

"I hooked up with Queen Sasha's favorite guard. Apparently, she felt slighted that he would have me but not her." Tameer blew gently into his cup. "I don't think she grasps the idea that a man might not be interested in women at all. Anyway, she found out and put a hit out on me. My guild saw it as an opportunity to oust me. They didn't appreciate the way I'd been running things for some time."

Leah leaned back in her chair. She'd heard rumors before they'd left town, that some of the Thieves Guild took issue with Tameer's policies about child labor. He'd banned training kids in the art of theft until they were at least ten. He still accepted the kids into the guild, but they were members in name only until they were old enough to grasp the weight of their decisions. Before the age of ten, the kids were housed, fed, protected, and cared for, but not trained. Many of the guild members felt like that was a waste of resources.

"So you got off and now they're trying to off you. It's kinda amusing, actually." Leah smirked behind her mug. The assassins and bounty hunters who had come to claim Tameer's corpse and the likely hefty fortune now tied to it hadn't been the best in Ravendale, but they had been decent. One of them had almost cut her. *Leah.* The highest-paid, most effective, and most sought-after assassin in the world! It was *almost* offensive.

"I'm glad you're enjoying my misery." Tameer pouted into his tea.

Leah leaned forward, taking his hands in hers and demanding his full attention. "Tam, you screwed up. It happens, especially when you're leading with the wrong head. But you aren't going to die. Not unless you keep drinking away my coin and passing out at the table like an old, land-locked pirate." She squeezed his hands to emphasize her words. "You are the most clever person I've ever met. If you'd give yourself five minutes to get acclimated, I bet you'd thrive here, too."

And that had been the end of it. Tameer sobered up and started helping her in the garden. Over the next few months, Leah watched their fellow townsfolk, learning their habits, studying their behavior, and eventually honing her niche in this new, slower-paced world.

By the end of the fourth month, Leah had claimed the role of town baker. It wasn't as high stakes as her previous position—world-renowned assassin—but it was something she was surprised to find she truly enjoyed.

Until that damned messenger arrived and turned their new life on its head. Now she needed to plan and carry out an assassination of the king, all while being stalked by a giant of a soldier. Madame Luck didn't appear to be on Leah's side anymore.

Shit.

Chapter 4

As much as she wanted to appear calm and unaffected, Leah slept like shit that night. Weird dreams about creepy eyes spying on her through the windows. Voices whispering just out of range so she couldn't understand them, but she *knew* they were plotting her demise. It was like her early days with the Assassin's Guild all over again.

She was up before the sun and had finished all the loaves of sourdough before Tameer rolled out of bed. His normally perfectly coiffed hair was a rat's nest over his puffy eyes.

"Geez, you look well-rested," she teased, tossing him a biscuit as he shuffled to the carafe of coffee waiting at the table.

"Screw you. Only a psychopath could sleep well knowing a highly trained soldier was here to hunt and likely kill them." Tameer poured himself a steaming cup of coffee, dropping three sugar cubes into it before inhaling deeply and taking that first blessed sip.

"First of all, he's not here to hunt or kill *you*. I don't see why you're so worried. You'll be fine either way."

Tameer looked at her, his mouth hanging open in what she could only describe as disbelief. Or perhaps awe at her clearly fearless exterior.

"You can't honestly think that I'd be ok without you. You aren't that dense or emotionally stunted, are you?"

Tameer set his cup down and crossed the room, pinning her with a very serious look. Leah tried to move away, put some distance between them. She needed space if she was going to do what she needed to do. She couldn't let him get in her head with all these emotions and shit.

He knew what she was doing, though. Damn him. He knew her too well and he kept moving closer. When she backed into the kitchen counter, Tameer placed his hands on either side of her, effectively trapping her.

"You are the most important person in my life," he began, his voice low as his eyes burned into hers. "You can be as flippant as you want about this, but know this: I love you and if anything happens to you, I will kill myself trying to avenge you."

Leah blinked several times, trying to hide the tears that threatened to overflow her lashes.

"If you want to act like this isn't a big deal, because you think it will keep me from worrying, fine, but I think we both know you aren't that naive. As long as this stalker is here, I'm going to worry, I'm going to lose sleep, and I'm going to watch you like a fucking hawk."

Wiping her eyes, Leah tried to swallow the emotion clogging her throat. "Tam, I..." she began, but the words wouldn't come.

Pulling her into a tight embrace, Tameer placed a firm kiss on the top of her head. "It's ok, Leah. I know you don't do emotions or displays of affection well. But don't go around expecting me to do the same."

A watery laugh escaped her lips as she leaned into his warmth. Leah would never be able to vocalize how she felt about Tameer, but she appreciated that he knew her heart, even if she couldn't say it.

They stood like that for a while, until the timer dinged and Tameer released his hold on her and retrieved the cookies from their wood-burning stove.

"Gods, these smell amazing," he said, effectively ending their emotional scene. Leah exhaled slowly, stuffing her emotions back into the steel lockbox she had deep in her chest.

"Those are just for us. I had some leftover batter, so I made a few extra." Leah nodded to the box on the counter tied with a forest green ribbon. Those were for the client. They'd be along to pick up their order in a few hours, but Leah had accidentally doubled the recipe and didn't want to just throw away the batter. The lavender cookies were some of her favorites. No reason to waste them because she'd been distracted.

"You had leftover batter?" Tameer raised an incredulous eyebrow. "I didn't think the great Leah was capable of making mistakes."

Leah chuckled but nodded. "It is rare, but it's possible. I'm only human."

Tameer scoffed at her bad joke. Leah was half-human, of course, but her fae genetics won out more often than not. The fact that she'd made a mistake while baking that morning had nothing to do with her parentage and everything to do with the knot of stress eating away at her insides. She hadn't been hunted in years. She didn't care for it.

The rest of the morning passed quickly with customers coming to place or pick up orders. As the sun began to sink beyond the horizon, Leah had almost managed to forget about the stranger. Until she looked out the window and saw him kneeling in her garden, browsing through her herbs.

"What the hells?" she muttered. Dropping the dough she'd been working and wiping her flour-covered hands on her apron, Leah double-checked the curved daggers that were sheathed at the base of her spine. Tameer often teased her about being armed all the time, even when baking in their home, but Leah felt naked without a blade. If he were here now, she'd rub it in his face. Being prepared is always better than being caught unaware.

Striding out the back door, Leah crossed the garden and practically shoved the man. To her annoyance, he barely moved.

"Who the hells are you and why are you in my garden?" she demanded, glaring down at him.

Slowly, her stalker brushed off his knees and rose to his full height.

Fuck. He was tall. Leah took a step back to avoid looking straight up while holding his glare.

He grabbed the back of his neck, looking almost sheepish as he studied her. If Leah didn't know better, she'd think he was trying to seduce her. But she was a trained killer. No soldier was going to pull one over on her. Even if he did have startlingly blue eyes and lips that were clearly meant for pleasure.

Stop that. Stay focused.

"Well?" she prompted, putting as much irritation and authority into her voice as she could.

"Apologies," he said in a rough voice. "I didn't mean to scare you."

Leah scoffed. "You most certainly did *not* scare me. You're trespassing. You're lucky I haven't slit your throat already."

He flinched at her words. Good. She was hoping they'd hit the mark. From this vantage point, she could clearly see the thin, jagged scar across his throat. Someone had already tried and failed to slit this man's throat. She wouldn't be so clumsy.

Ash didn't appreciate her disrespectful attitude. No one dared comment on his scar. Certainly not some half-fae murderess.

He was only *mostly* sure she was half-fae. Her skin was too fair to be full-blooded fae. Her ears weren't pointed and her nose was more of a button than the elongated, haughty thing that usually featured front and center in the faces of full-blooded fae. But her hair and that arrogance were definitely trademark fae.

Swallowing his instincts, Ash tried to appear as friendly as possible. He'd been trained to kill in a thousand different ways, but the art of seduction was largely lost on him. He didn't typically see the point of such soft action when one hard hit could solve the problem quicker and easier. However, after a thorough—if distant—inspection of the half-fae's home last night, Ash knew he wouldn't be able to sneak up on this creature. He'd have to get her to drop her guard, even if only a little.

Ash blinked slowly, like the courtesans did when they wanted things from the king. He felt insanely awkward doing it, but he was rewarded by a small smile tugging at the assassin's soft, pink lips.

Soft? Why the hells was he thinking about the texture of her lips? Gods, he needed to stay focused. Ash had never let a woman distract him before. He sure as hells wasn't going to start now.

Clearing his throat, he tried again. "Apologies, miss. I was told you were the best baker in town. I was hoping to place an order. I got distracted by your garden." He motioned to the raised bed directly beside him. "You've got some interesting plants here. Belladonna? Nightshade? Oleander and Lily of the Valley? Those are all quite deadly, aren't they? Seems an odd choice for the town's baker."

The assassin blinked a moment, seeming a bit thrown by his accurate identifications of the tools of her trade. Poison. A coward's weapon if there ever was one.

"I'm impressed," she hedged, avoiding answering his question directly. "Most people don't know those plants. Fewer still can identify them on sight that easily. Tell me, trespasser, what do you do for a living?" She had the gall to question him so blatantly. As though he were a common criminal like herself?

Grinding his teeth to keep from saying something he shouldn't, Ash shrugged as casually as he could. "Bit of this. Bit of that." He'd heard that answer enough times from criminals on the street. He knew it would be sufficient.

She chuckled, a sparkle of amusement lighting up her eyes, as she nodded and motioned for him to follow her.

Ash was a bit thrown by the sudden change in her attitude, but he couldn't deny he enjoyed the sound of the small laugh that had escaped her alluring lips.

Gods, take me. He was getting sucked in by her fae magic. That must be what was going on. He would never be attracted to a criminal otherwise. He came here to seduce her, not the other way around. Internally chastising himself, he followed her over to a stone bench that sat against the house, looking out at the garden.

She took a seat on the stone, crossing her legs under her and looking far too childlike and innocent. She was a killer. He could never forget that fact. She smiled up at him and patted the stone beside her.

Awkwardly, as though his joints were beginning to rust, Ash moved to join her, leaning against the back of the house as casually as he dared. She shifted in her seat to face him, staring at him as though she might see directly into his soul. It was very unsettling, although he refused to let that show.

"What can I do you for?" She said after several long moments. "Are you here for my baked goods? Or something more salacious?" The last word came out as a breathy whisper. Much to Ash's frustration, his body responded to her sultry tone and the warm breath of her words on his neck.

She was too close. Far too close. When had she moved? She was practically on top of him. Before he could stop himself, Ash bolted to his feet, taking several steps away from the bench and the harlot atop it.

Cackling, the murderess raised her hands in defense, tears of humor threatening her brilliant purple eyes.

Gods, he fucking hated fae.

Leah couldn't help it. The man was clearly the most buttoned-up, self-righteous, pious son of a bitch to ever venture into Vexia. Obviously a soldier, it amused her that he first attempted to seduce her—rather sloppily—and then tried to convince her he was a criminal. It was just so damn laughable. Leah imagined the man had never so much as stolen a slice of bread. It was cute that he thought he could fool her though.

"Oh, come on. There's no need to act so scandalized." Leah tucked her hands into her lap, beaming up at the man as a brilliant flush reddened his battle-worn face. He really was sexy, if he didn't have that high-and-mighty attitude. Hells, he might even be fun if he'd just lighten up a bit.

Still, he'd clearly come here with some nefarious plans in mind for her, and she needed to get to the bottom of it.

"So, darlin', what do you need? Bread? Cookies? A poison so efficient it will kill your mark in a matter of heartbeats and leave no trace? Or would you rather something slow? Make them suffer for a while, dragging it out to ensure they know exactly who killed them and why? I can do it all."

The man seemed thrown by her blunt words, but Leah knew his type. He was either here to kill her, or here to kill someone else and try to blame her. It had all been done before and she'd always come out on top. She was tired of these games, so she decided to get straight to the point.

"I don't know who you are, but you're definitely not a criminal. We criminals are quite adept at identifying each other, and you are not one of us. In fact, I'd bet my life that you are a soldier. Probably for that king I was hired to kill."

He balked. As though he was shocked that she'd be so glib and forthcoming about the assassination she'd recently been commissioned to commit. When the offer had come through, Leah hadn't been sure she wanted to come out of retirement to do it. She had no love for the king, hells, she'd heard some horror stories about the things he'd done, but Leah was enjoying her retirement. However, between Tameer telling her she couldn't do it, and this asshat trying to kill her before she got the chance to make up her own mind, Leah felt compelled to take the job. It was petty of her, she knew it, but it was in her blood. When someone told her she couldn't or shouldn't do something, she *needed* to prove them wrong.

"You're a murderer." The man glared at her. He pulled a dagger from his boot, pointing it threateningly at her. "You are a vile temptress, half-blood trash. I should kill you where you stand."

"First of all, I'm sitting." Leah gestured to herself. "Secondly, that's not very polite. I didn't call you names. Didn't your mother teach you anything?" Leah had heard all those comments a hundred thousand times before. She prided herself on embodying the insults, living up to people's bigoted impressions of her. Until she ended their worthless lives.

He was practically shaking with rage. Interesting. Perhaps her comment about his mother had hit a soft spot. She'd remember that.

"Listen, soldier boy, if you are here to kill me, you're wasting your time and mine. If you are here to hire me—as you clearly aren't capable of stealth at even the most rudimentary level—you are welcome to join me for a cuppa and some fresh scones." With that, she rose from the bench and ventured back into her house, leaving the stranger standing awkwardly—and a bit angrily—in the middle of her garden.

Chapter 5

Gods, that woman. That *woman*. She was so arrogant, self-righteous, cocky, and flippant. Ash wanted to put her over his knee. If she was going to behave like a child, she should be punished like one.

He paced in the garden for several minutes. Trying to regain his composure. He should have just killed her. Why didn't he? Shaking his head, as though to rid himself of these thoughts, he shoved the blade back into the sheath in his boot and stomped into her house.

It was nothing like he'd expected when he pictured an assassin's home. It was bright, colorful, and smelled mouthwateringly sweet. The scent of fresh bread and baked goods nearly knocked him on his ass. The assassin turned to face him, a large mixing bowl clutched to her amble chest as she worked the mixture with a wooden spoon.

"Ah! Look who finally got over himself enough to come inside. I thought I was going to have to throw treats at you until you gave in." A shit-eating grin was plastered over her face. He hadn't even been outside that long.

He opened his mouth to protest, but she shooed him off with her batter-covered spoon.

"Have a seat. The kettle's on. Tea will be ready shortly. Scones are in the basket on the table. Under the linen." She turned away then, setting her bowl on the counter and adding some spices to the mix. "You never said who you want me to kill."

Ash glared at the back of her rose gold head. "I don't want you to kill anyone." He took a seat at her table, crossing his arms over his chest.

"Well then, it's odd that you came seeking an assassin."

She was so damned snarky. Ash had never hit a woman before—outside of battle—but the idea of spanking this one for her insolence was becoming more and more appealing.

"I came here to kill you," Ash growled, all pretense having vanished as she continued to prod him.

"Well, you're doing a bang-up job so far," she said, tossing an exaggerated wink over her shoulder at him. She pulled a large metal sheet out from one of the cabinets and began scooping dollops of the batter onto the sheet.

Ash ground his teeth as he watched her work. He was supposed to be endearing himself to her, at least enough for her to drop her guard and one or two of her house wards. Why was he being so honest with her now? He needed to get a handle on himself.

"So tell me, soldier boy, why do you want to kill me?" She opened the oven and placed the baking sheet inside.

"You were hired to kill the king. It is my job to protect him." Fuck. Why? He hadn't meant to say any of that out loud.

"Oh, and you love this king of yours, do you? You are protecting him out of the goodness of your heart and an unwavering sense of loyalty?" The assassin took the now whistling kettle from the stove, grabbed two teacups, and joined him at the table.

"No. I ha-" Ash slammed his mouth shut. What the actual hells was going on?

The assassin smiled broadly. "Clever thing, runes. Did you know if you carve the right ones, in just the right order, you can make it impossible for guests to lie? It's quite handy when dealing with would-be killers and potential enemies."

Ash clenched his jaw so hard he was sure he'd crack a tooth. He should have known better. He ventured into a viper's nest without any thought to caution or the traps that might lay in wait.

"Let me get this straight," the assassin went on as she set their tea to steep and selected a scone from the basket. "You hate your king, but you are here to kill me so I don't kill him? You must have a very stubborn sense of duty, soldier boy."

Blowing on her tea, she took a tentative sip. She made a face, then added four sugar cubes to the small mug. Ash stared at her as blankly as possible, trying to fight the compulsion to tell her everything as she tore her scone into bite-size pieces and tossed them confidently into her mouth.

"Come on, you can tell me anything. Who am I gonna tell, any-way? Who would believe me?" Her voice was melodic. Hypnotic. Ash ran a hand through his hair, trying to wipe her influence from his mind. "It's all right, darling," she practically purred. "You can talk to me. I'm here to help."

Ash wanted to tell her everything. He wanted to pour his heart out to her, so she could know him and maybe even love him.

Wait, *what?!*

"Stop that!" He snapped at her, jumping up from the table and putting as much distance between them as the small kitchen would allow.

Her cackling laugh was all the confirmation he needed. The damn half-fae bitch was using *magic* on him. Trying to manipulate his emotions and con him into revealing his secrets. It wouldn't work. He couldn't let it. She couldn't know what he had planned, it would ruin everything.

"All right, all right. I'll stop, as long as you promise to be honest. If I catch a hint of a lie, I'll turn you into my love-sick puppy and you won't be able to stop me."

In a blink, Ash felt a weight on his mind lift and his vision cleared. The room, which had looked magnificent and vibrant a moment ago, looked more worn and hard now. The countertops that were shiny and flawless now appeared faded and chipped in several spots. Not to mention covered in flour. And the over-whelmingly sweet smell lightened to a more yeasty, warm scent with just a hint of sugary sweetness.

Ash glared at the assassin temptress. She, on the other hand, looked entirely calm and collected, sitting cross-legged in her chair, sipping her tea with an air of confidence that grated on him more than he wanted to acknowledge.

"You gonna tell me why you're trying to kill me? Or is this a guessing game? I'm up for games, but if we're doing that, then I have some ground rules." She raised her hand and started listing off her supposed rules. "One: No lies, obviously. Two: No questions about my parents. That's more because it's annoying than anything since I don't know anything about them. Three: You have to sit down. My neck is already getting tired of staring up like this. And four: when my partner returns, you have to be a perfect gentleman. If he finds out I let a wannabe killer into our home again, he's gonna be pissed."

Leah was hoping the soldier would be gone before Tameer returned, but clearly, Madame Luck wasn't on her side today. She held the man's stare for a moment, watching him internally debate her rules. He'd agree to them, of course. He came here to kill her, but he hadn't yet. He'd had the opportunity. Leah hadn't tried controlling him when they were outside and he hadn't made any serious attempt to end her life then. Granted, when he came in, she had glamored him some, but she did that with every new guest in their home. Especially highly trained military types. Not that they got a lot of those around Vexia.

"Tell me, soldier boy, why did you come all the way to Vexia to kill me? Why not hire your own assassin? Or send a battalion if I'm such a threat?"

"What did you call this place?" His question caught her off-guard a bit. Not the context of it—people always got the name of the town wrong—but his tone had changed. Less combative.

"ve-HAY-ah. I know, I know. It looks like vex-ee-AH. I don't know why it's called that, but any local could happily give you a history lesson, if you're interested." Leah recalled when she first moved here, she'd mispronounced the name once and gotten an earful from the butcher. Apparently, his family had been here since the founding, four generations back. He was quick to correct people, even though most still got it wrong. "Let's start off easy," Leah said, getting them back on track. "My name is Leah. What's yours?"

Soldier boy clenched his jaw, seeming to debate whether or not to answer her honestly, or at all. Finally, he exhaled a sigh of frustration, nodded to himself, and joined her back at the table. "Ash."

"It's a pleasure to meet you, Ash. I'm still gonna call you 'soldier boy' though. It's more fun." That earned her another annoyed glare. A grin tugged at her lips, but she tried to quash it. If she mocked him too much, he'd refuse to play her game and they were just getting started.

"Who hired you to kill the king?" His voice was rough, but not unappealing. It had a smokey edge to it that Leah found almost pleasant.

"I can't tell you that. But I can say that it's a long time coming. That king of yours is a violent, abusive son of a bitch. He needs to be put down like the rabid dog he is." She watched his reaction to her words, trying to get a read on him. He didn't flinch at her description of the king, or move to defend the man. "You already know all this, don't you?"

Ash's refusal to answer was all the confirmation she needed. He knew his king was a monster. He took a scone from the basket and began tearing it into crumbs. He hadn't taken a sip of his tea either. He didn't trust her food or drink, despite the fact that he'd seen her eating and drinking the same things. It was mildly offensive but also entirely justified. She was a poisoner, after all. Food and drink in her presence should always be suspect.

"If you know he's so terrible, why would you try and stop me?"

He was quiet for a long time. Leah was starting to wonder if he was refusing to answer still, but something in him seemed to click and when he spoke, she was stunned.

"He's my father. I'm the bastard son of the king and Captain of the King's Guard. It's my job to protect that man, even if he's as vile as you claim. Or worse." His voice trailed off as his mind seemed to wander somewhere else. Clearing his throat, he refocused. "My mother is dead because of him. I can't let you kill him because avenging her death is my duty."

Chapter 6

Shit. He hadn't meant to say that out loud. The weight of her charms was still absent, so Ash trusted that the murderess—Leah—hadn't put another spell on him. So why the hells was he still spilling his guts to her? He hadn't told anyone about his mother. Not even his most trusted guards. He sure as shit shouldn't be revealing his weaknesses and true motives to a known killer.

She said nothing for a while, watching him with an annoyingly pensive look on her face. She was assessing him. Who gave her the right?

Ash leaned back in his chair, arms across his chest once more, as he attempted to calm his mind and regain control of his mouth.

"All right, I'll help you." Leah nodded and leaned back in her own chair.

"Come again?" he asked. His voice was more of a growl than he intended. Ash took a deep breath before he spoke again. "I don't want your help."

"Want it or not, you clearly need it." The flippant little assassin tossed her pink hair confidently over her shoulder and grabbed another scone from the basket. "You couldn't even sneak up on me. How the hells do you think you're gonna kill a king?"

Ash stared at her, open-mouthed and thoroughly irate. "I don't want your help," he ground out again.

Leah rose from the table and sashayed over to a cabinet beside the ice box. "Soldier boy, you *need* my help if you want to kill a king in cold blood and get away with it." She rummaged through a thousand vials within the cabinet, coming back with three small, dark bottles. "Killing as a soldier is public and socially acceptable. You don't have to be stealthy. If you kill someone when you're dressed like that," she gestured to his entire body, "people assume the person you took out deserved it. The entire country knows the king is a piece of shit, but they'll still cut off your head if you get caught."

Ash schooled his face, refusing to let her see the effect her words were having on him. He hadn't really thought this through yet. He'd come here to stop a threat to the king and his own plans to take the man from this earth, but damn him—and her—he hadn't put any thought into *how* he'd kill that bastard and get away with it.

Ash supposed he didn't really care if he got away with it. Mother was all he had, and she was long gone.

Leah set the bottles down on the table, then turned back and retrieved the baking sheet from her oven, setting it on the stovetop to cool.

"Here's what I'm thinking. A mixture of those two," she nodded to the two green glass vials, "will make him sick to his stomach. He'll be shitting himself within an hour. When he excuses himself to hide out in his chambers, you can either give him some of this one," lifting the black glass vial as she spoke, "maybe in a glass of wine?—or you can kill him in whatever brutal way you see fit."

Ash shifted in his chair. He was discussing treason with a known killer like it was a casual coffee shop conversation. He ran a hand through his shaggy hair, wondering how he'd even got to this point.

"It's all right, soldier boy. If you don't want to go through with it, I'm not gonna tell anyone you were thinking about it. Who would I tell anyway?" Leah offered him a small, kind smile. Ash was shocked to realize that he truly believed her. She would keep his confidence. "There's also the option where you let me do what I was hired to do and we both get what we want: payday for me and a dead daddy for you."

"Gods, do you have to be so callous? I was almost starting to think you were a normal person. Taking someone's life shouldn't be about a payday."

"Should it be about revenge, then? Is that the morally acceptable reason to kill someone?"

She had him there. He wasn't any better than her, his motives were just as selfish.

"Look, soldier boy,"

He groaned, cutting her off. "Can you stop calling me that? Ash. Just call me Ash."

"No can do, soldier boy," she grinned proudly. "Soldier boy is far more fitting and I've already become attached to it."

"I don't want you attached to anything about it or me," he grumbled.

"Too late, darlin'!" she cheered. "We're plotting an assassination together. We're basically besties now. Don't tell Tam."

"Don't tell Tam what?" A man's voice called from the front door.

Shit. Ash really didn't want another witness to his ineptitude.

"We have company," Leah announced as Tameer hung his cloak on the hook beside the door and turned to face her. *Please don't be mad*, she thought. Leah hated when she and Tam fought.

"Oh yeah?" Curiosity lifted a single eyebrow until he looked at their table and saw Ash sitting there. His expression shifted quickly from intrigued to barely contained anger. "Leah," his voice held an edge of rage while his eyes stayed firmly fixed on their guest. "Can I speak to you in private?"

Yeah, he was pissed. She nodded and followed Tameer into the next room, where they wouldn't be overheard but she could still keep an eye on Ash. He was a soldier and apparently a very honest one, but she still didn't know if he was trustworthy.

"What the fuck are you doing? That's the asshole who was stalking us at the bar the other night. Why the hells is he in our *home*?"

Leah tried to place a gentle hand on Tameer's shoulder but he quickly shrugged her off. "I know who he is. He was in the garden this morning, so I confronted and glamored him. He's not here to kill us. He might be here to hire me though..."

Tam froze in place at that. Leah watched as several emotions crossed over his face. Confusion and distrust being the two most prominent. "Explain."

Leah wanted to tell her friend everything, but she gave her word to Ash that she wouldn't reveal his plans, and she felt compelled to keep that promise. "Why don't you join us and hear him out?" she asked instead.

"Are you serious? He's a fucking soldier for the king you're planning to kill. This is easily the stupidest thing you've ever done, Leah. And that's *really* saying something."

She would rather take a punch to the ovaries than hear Tameer's disappointment. Especially when he knew exactly which buttons to push to emphasize his feelings and drive home his point.

"Fuck you," she seethed. "Don't you fucking dare come in here and start questioning *my* choices. I'm the *only* reason you're alive right now." She turned on her heel and left him standing there, stewing in his ignorance and misplaced anger.

That was the guy who'd carried her out of the bar. The one who'd had his hands all over her. Ash felt an unreasonable amount of rage toward the man, although he refused to look too closely at it. He had no reason to feel anything but disgust about this half-fae assassin or her partner. She was nothing to Ash. A mission. Killing her was meant to be his mission.

How had he gotten so off task so quickly?

"Sorry about that," Leah said as she sauntered back into the room. The sway of her hair and hips was nearly hypnotic as Ash watched her retrieve a book from the counter. "Where were we?"

Ash blinked, trying to clear his head and shake loose the highly inappropriate thoughts that crept in as he watched her move.

"You ok, soldier boy?" she asked, taking her seat across the table from him. There was genuine concern in her expression. He'd come here to kill her and now *she* was worried about *his* well-being?

What the actual fuck?

"Are you magicking me again?" Ash demanded. He wiped his face, as though that action could wipe away all the thoughts of his hands on her body instead of that angry asshole in the next room.

"What? No. I told you I wouldn't and I meant it." She seemed legitimately offended by his question. That surprised Ash more than anything. He would have thought an assassin would be used to people not trusting them. "Listen, I know Tam came in all abrasive and like a general dick, but he doesn't speak for me and I'd like to still help you, if you're interested."

Correction. *That* surprised Ash more than anything. Dumbfounded, he blinked several times before being able to put a response together. "Um, right. Like I said, I didn't come here for your help."

"Right, you came here to kill me, then you were gonna get yourself killed trying to do my job."

Normally, Ash appreciated bluntness and honesty, but damn if hers wasn't just a little too brutal.

"Soldier boy. Ash. I want that fucker dead. I've been hired to do the job, which is just an extra little bonus as far as I'm concerned. I'm happy to do it solo, but if you want to be involved, I'll need to adjust my plan. If you want the killing blow, that's fine by me. I tend not to be around when my marks die anyway. It's why I'm still alive." Leah held his stare, a look of confidence and compassion in her eyes that threw him almost as much as the little thrill he'd felt when she'd called him by his name.

"I don't like this," he grumbled. Breaking their stare, he picked at the scone he'd been actively not eating for the last hour. The tea had long gone cold, but he still hadn't had a sip. Ash had no reason to trust this assassin but damn him if he wasn't starting to.

Leah rose from the table, grabbed a large plate from one of the cabinets, and began placing the cookies on it as she spoke. "I know this is all new territory for you, but I'm quite skilled, as I'm sure you've heard. This man killed your mother and countless others. He's had ample time to change his ways and become a decent human and ruler. He makes the selfish, violent choice every time. Killing him is the humane thing to do. It will save countless more lives from the terror he brings. Not to mention, avenging your mom is quite the noble cause, if you ask me."

"I didn't. But thank you, I guess." He hated how logical her argument was. He hated even more how much he agreed with her. "Fine. You can help me."

"Yay!" she cheered, practically dancing as she carried the plate of cookies over to the table. "Let's celebrate. Then we can plot some treason before I have to start in on the loaves of bread for tomorrow."

Chapter 7

"What are you doing?" Leah shoved Tameer away. "You can't put arsenic in the *sourdough starter*. You'll kill my food baby before I even get started."

Tameer shrugged. "I'm helping."

It had been a few days since Leah agreed to work with Ash. She'd hoped Tameer would get over it and decide to help her, but clearly, that was not the case.

Leah huffed, scooping up the jar of her starter and cradling it to her chest. "Helping who? Because you sure as shit aren't helping me if you kill my baby." She carefully tucked it away in a cabinet and turned back to glare at him.

"I'm helping protect *you* from yourself. You can't go around poisoning kings, Leah. And teaming up with a soldier from the King's Guard? You'll get us both arrested and executed. Treason isn't something royals take lightly." His dry tone grated on her almost as much as his blatant attempts at ruining her starter.

"You can disagree with my actions all you want, but leave Buffy out of this. There's no need to poison her just because you're upset with me."

"Don't you understand that what you're being asked to do... it's going to change everything! And probably not in a good way." Tameer threw himself onto the chair in her kitchen.

She studied him for a moment, then said, "Do you like the king?"

Tameer laughed indignantly. "Like him? Hells no. I don't think anyone likes him. He's killed off a new queen every year for as long as I can remember. He's a violent, power-mad psychopath."

Leah nodded in agreement. "So killing him would save an indefinite number of lives. Not to mention sparing all those in his employ that he takes for his pleasure, regardless of their desire or consent. I'm doing a *service* to the people, Tameer. Can't you see that?"

"Oh yes, I can tell your motives are purely altruistic. How could I have missed that before?" His deadpan tone dripped with sarcasm.

Leah grinned widely. "No reason why I shouldn't get paid for my efforts. It's not easy being the best assassin in the country. I should be properly reimbursed for my time and energy."

"And this guard? What's his deal? Why does he want to kill the king? Are you sure this isn't some elaborate plot to catch you in the act and have you executed for attempted murder?"

With a grimace, Leah rubbed her temples. They'd been over this a thousand times but Tam just wouldn't drop it. "I already told you, his reasons are *his* to share or keep. I can tell you—like I've been saying for the last few days—his motives are pure. He's not going to betray me."

Tameer glared at her but thankfully dropped that argument. "Do you even know who hired you this time?" He tried again. "I hate when you go in blind, working for a friend of a friend or some shit."

Leah glanced down at her boots. She didn't quite know how to tell him, although it really wasn't fair of her to keep such vital information from her partner.

"Leah," Tameer said, an edge of chastisement in his voice. "Who hired you? Who is so willing to risk your life for their own gain?"

Leah swiped her foot back and forth across the ground before her, making a smooth arch in the dirt floor. Not daring to look up and see the judgment in his face. "Just promise you won't get mad, ok?"

"I most certainly will not." Tameer's voice shifted from chastising to barely contained anger. He knew. She didn't have to say it. He already knew.

"Queen Irena."

Over the course of the last few days, Ash had changed his mind about a hundred times. It was crazy for him to willingly work with an assassin. It was crazier still for him to think he could kill the king on his own and survive the encounter.

But trusting a killer? Gods, take him. He didn't know what the right choice was. He needed the man dead, and it *needed* to be at his hand, but fuck him. Everything seemed dramatically more complicated now, after his conversation with Leah, than it had seemed before.

Before though, he hadn't had a plan, just blind rage and a burning need for vengeance. Leah had a plan. A good one, honestly, which shocked him more than it should have. Hells, she was a world-class assassin who'd never missed a mark or gotten caught.

It would have been more surprising if her plan had been shit. Like his.

However, now that things were in motion, Ash couldn't shake the gnawing feeling in his gut that something was going to go terribly, terribly wrong. There were still too many unknowns. Too many factors outside of his control. Too many ways things could go awry. He hated it. Not to mention, once the king was dead, the entire country would be in upheaval for a while. Likely, the queen would step in and take over, as the king had no legitimate heirs, but there would be a period of extreme unrest and quite possibly a coup attempt or two.

Ash walked aimlessly around the small town, nodding to the occasional vendor, but largely lost in thought, so much so that he didn't even see Tameer until he ran smack into the man and nearly knocked him on his ass.

"Shit," Ash swore, reaching out to catch him before Tameer fell to the dirt. "I'm sorry. I wasn't looking and I just... shit. Are you ok?"

Tameer jerked his arm out of Ash's grasp and glared at him. *If looks could kill...*

"I'm fine," he grumbled, hate filtered in his words and his gaze. "Why are you even fucking here?"

Ash shrugged. "I went for a walk to clear my head."

"No," Tameer interjected. "Why are you *here*? Why are you in Vexia? You got her to agree to do this insane job. You're going to get her killed and you're still hanging around like a lost puppy."

Ash clenched his jaw, flexing his fists to keep from punching that man before him. "I'm not a lost puppy. I'm a captain in the King's Guard and I deserve more respect than you or your *partner* have bothered to show me."

"Respect is *earned*, pretty boy," Tameer sneered. "You haven't done shit to earn my respect. Hells, you came here to kill her. You don't have my trust and you sure as hells don't deserve my respect." He spat on the ground at Ash's feet, a challenge in his words and his glare. He was itching for a fight, and honestly, Ash was more than willing to give it to him.

But that wouldn't be prudent or productive. As much as he wanted to knock that man to the ground once more, Ash knew it wouldn't improve their relationship. Loathe as he was to admit it, he needed Tameer on his side—or at least not fighting against him—if he and Leah were going to accomplish their mission.

He took a step back and several deep breaths before he spoke again. "I think we got off on the wrong foot."

Tameer had the nerve to laugh at Ash. "You think so?" he asked with a condescending smirk. "You came here to hunt down and kill my *best friend*. I don't know how you convinced her to trust you, but I'm not going to be so easily swayed."

Gods, this man was infuriating. He could see why Leah liked him so much, though. The man was loyal to a fault.

"Can I buy you a drink?"

Tameer seemed thrown by the non sequitur but quickly recovered. "It's not going to change my mind about you, but if you wanna waste your coin, I'm happy to drink for free."

The walk to the tavern was short but painfully awkward. Ash was relieved when they finally reached the tavern doors and were greeted by the stench of sweat, stale beer, and piss.

It was mildly comforting to know that no matter where in the realm you were, taverns always smelled the same.

Gross, but consistent.

Tameer sidled up to the bar, took a seat, and waved Geoffree over. "Two beers," he said. "On him." Tameer tossed a look over his shoulder at Ash.

Geoffree raised a curious eyebrow but didn't say a word as he dispensed two frothy beers from the tap, placing the tankards on the bar.

Ash took the empty seat beside Tameer and nodded a quick thanks to Geoffree. Turning to Tameer, he said, "What can I do to help you trust me? Or at least make you hate me a little less? If we're supposed to work together, it would be best if neither of us had to worry about being stabbed in the back."

Tameer took a long pull from his mug, leaving a mockable foam mustache on his upper lip. Under other circumstances, Ash might have teased the man about it, but considering he was trying to make peace, insults were likely not the best route.

Tameer wiped his mouth with the back of his hand, shifting in his seat to face Ash directly. "You can tell me the real reason you want to do this. Leah is convinced that your motives are pure, but she won't tell me anything else. Tell me why you want to," he looked over his shoulder and dropped his voice to a whisper as he said, "kill the king."

That challenge was back in his eyes, even as his voice was barely audible.

Ash schooled his face as he processed what Tameer had just said. Leah had kept her word. She hadn't revealed his truths to her partner, even though it had clearly created a rift between them. It was a bit shocking to learn that the assassin was, in fact, a woman of her word.

Ash took a drink of his own beer, stalling as he internally debated whether it was worth it to reveal himself to this man who clearly hated him—with good reason, but still.

"You want my trust and respect? I want your honesty." Tameer made an annoyingly good point. Ash couldn't expect to be trusted if their entire relationship was based on secrets and lies.

Internally sighing, Ash leaned closer to avoid being overheard as he revealed his full truth to the assassin's partner. He hated giving this man power over him, but he needed to earn his trust and the fastest way to do that was through honesty.

He sat back to see a look of pure shock on Tameer's face. "You've got to be shitting me. He's your…" He trailed off, thankfully not finishing the sentence aloud. "And he killed your mom? When? How?"

Gods, take him. Ash didn't want to relay that story. He hadn't even told Leah that part of it. he shifted uncomfortably on the barstool, taking several long drinks before finally speaking. "He didn't do it directly. He's too powerful to bother getting his hands dirty. But when he found out about my existence, he sent some of his guards to arrest my mother on some bullshit charge. He'd intended to imprison her and kill me, but she fought back. She wasn't a trained warrior, obviously, but she was fierce. She took a couple of the guards with her to the afterlife. I didn't want to leave her." The words caught in Ash's mouth, emotion clogging his throat. He swallowed a few times before finishing the story. "She'd hidden me under the floorboards so I heard the whole thing. The guards tore the house up looking for me, but I stayed frozen and silent. It was days before I came out from that hiding place. My mother lay pale and broken on the floor. They'd taken the dead guards with them and left her for the rats."

The image was still burned in his mind, nearly twenty years later. He saw her face as clearly as he saw his own. Eyes wide with fear as she lay in a dried puddle of her own blood. He could never seem to get that picture from his mind.

Blinking quickly, he took a swig of his beer and refocused his attention on the present.

"That," he said to Tameer with as much steel in his voice as he could muster, "is why I need that man dead at my feet."

Chapter 8

It was well after dark and Leah was beginning to wonder if Tameer was going to come home at all. Maybe he'd found comfort—or at least a distraction—with someone at the tavern and wouldn't be gracing her with his angry presence this evening after all. She hated being at odds with him, but she was doing this job. It needed to be done and she was the most equipped to accomplish it and live through the experience.

Plus, Irena needed her help.

Leah, Tameer, and Irena had grown up together. She was the girl Leah had first killed to protect. That action had set her on this path and Leah didn't know who she'd be if it hadn't been for that night, killing Shithead and getting Irena off the streets.

It should have been surprising when the king went to the local orphanage to find his latest bride, but after he killed the third one for not producing a male heir, families of repute stopped sending their daughters to Mistfall. He'd been forced to look elsewhere. Irena was twenty-four now and worked as a caretaker at the or-phanage. When the king had come through, looking for a child bride, she'd placed herself in his path and flirted herself into a death sentence in an effort to protect the children.

That was nine months ago. Irena hadn't borne the king a child yet, but she was due any day now. She'd contacted Leah in a last-ditch effort to keep herself and her unborn child safe from the monster that was her husband.

If anyone else had attempted to bring her out of retirement, Leah would have told them to fuck off and live with their choices. But Irena was the purest soul to ever escape the slums of Ravendale. She deserved a chance to grow old and watch her child do the same.

Tameer knew and understood that. Leah thought that flawless logic was part of the reason Tameer was so pissed at her. She was going to do this job and he couldn't stop her because he didn't really *want* to. He loved Irena as much as she did. They were their own little family and they had to protect each other.

A loud clatter from outside startled Leah from her memories. She'd been mindlessly kneading dough on the countertop so her hands were a bit sticky. Not ideal for defending one's self, but she'd been in worse situations. She quickly stuck her hands in the open flour bag, drying as much of the sticky dough as possible, double-checked that her blades were still easily accessible at the base of her spine, and stalked silently across the room to peer out the window of their front door.

What the hells?

Ash was drunk. He wasn't entirely sure how that had happened, but as he and Tameer stumbled down the path to Leah's front door, he leaned heavily on the man to stay upright. The only problem was that Tameer was just as intoxicated as he was. In moments, they were rolling on the dirt path, laughing uncontrollably as they struggled to find their footing again.

In the back of his mind, Ash chastised himself for being so sloppy and unprofessional, but he'd long since lost any semblance of self-control. Reliving the story of his mother's death opened a floodgate in his mind and he'd attempted to drown it out with a combination of beer, whisky, and gin.

Obviously, that hadn't worked out.

"Well, this is unexpected." There was a hit of humor in her voice as Leah stood in the doorway, arms crossed as though she were trying to convey a look of disappointment or disapproval.

"Hush, you." Tameer stumbled to the door. "Get outta the way. We need sustenance!"

Ash cackled at the way Tameer spoke. He cried for sustenance the way warriors cheered before charging into battle.

Leah grunted as Tameer pushed past her. "Rude! You could just ask, you know." She turned to eye Ash curiously. "Need any help there, soldier boy?"

He hadn't realized he was still lying on the path until she was standing over him. Gods, she was magnificent. Her long, wavy pink hair was coiled into a bun at the base of her skull, but fly-aways framed her face making her look like an angel with a rose gold halo.

Without warning, Ash rolled to his side and vomited.

Leah gagged. She'd been around a lot of disgusting things in her life. You'd think she would be immune to all bodily functions. Nope. People vomiting always made her want to throw up as well. It was one of the reasons she got into slow-acting poisons. It gave her plenty of time to get away before the gross things started.

She jumped back several feet as Ash emptied his gut onto her nice dirt path. Taking several deep breaths, she fought her own nausea and moved to kneel behind him, stroking his back as she'd done numerous times for Tameer over the years.

Ash groaned in appreciation—or perhaps defeat? Once he'd finished expelling everything he'd ingested that night, he looked like he was about to pass out in the grass.

"Oh, no. We need to get you inside first. You can't sleep out here. Drunken soldiers on my front walk will discourage customers and I've got a big order tomorrow." Leah rolled him over as slowly as she could, then hooked her arms around his chest. Well, she tried to anyway. He was far too broad for her to successfully wrap her arms around him completely. Grunting, she pulled him into a seated position, then sat back and waited. If he was going to vomit again, she didn't want it to be all over her. She wouldn't be able to quell her own nausea if he ruined her favorite apron.

After a few moments, when it was clear the nausea wasn't going to take him again, Leah straddled his lap, took his face in her flour-covered hands, and tilted his head until they were eye to eye. "Listen, big fella, I'm gonna need your help. I'm strong, but I'm not *that* strong. You have to stand. I'll help you to the house, but you have to get on your feet."

His eyes were unfocused. Leah wasn't entirely sure he'd even heard her, much less understood her words, but a moment later, he was shifting and slowly working himself to his knees and subsequently his feet.

Leah quickly jumped to his side, draping his arm across her shoulders as she wrapped her arms around him and took as much of his weight as she could.

"Fuck! What have they been feeding you?" she grumbled when he leaned into her and she practically collapsed under him.

"Sorry," he slurred. "I like to eat."

No shit. Leah marveled at the feel of him against her. With one arm wrapped around his back and the other pressed firmly into his chest to keep him upright, Leah could feel the hard plains of coiled muscle underneath his tunic. He'd seemed big in her kitchen before, but now, feeling the heat of his body pressed against hers, Leah was nearly overwhelmed by the size of him. He was all taut muscle and undeniable strength.

And hot. Really fucking hot.

Stop that, she chided herself. She was *not* going to let this sudden closeness develop into anything. She didn't have time for distractions. Hells, she was supposed to be planning an assassination, not feeling up the guard who'd come to kill her.

They moved slowly and gracelessly into her house. Tameer was at the dining table, using one of her day-old loaves of bread as a pillow. Great, he was passed out and would be utterly useless. Fuck.

At least he's using one of the day-olds and not a fresh loaf, she thought flippantly.

With as much care as she could, Leah guided Ash down the hall to her bedroom. She considered taking him to Tameer's room and letting the two of them share a bed to sleep off their idiotic male bonding ritual, but she decided against it. Ash could have her bed, just this once. She'd move Tam to his room next and sleep on the couch herself. She had to wake early anyway. The poison for the king needed to steep in the full moonlight to be most effective, but she'd need to get it back in the dark cabinet before the sun's light could diminish the potency.

They better appreciate this shit in the morning, she thought to herself.

After gently coaxing Ash into her bed, Leah threw a blanket over his large body and tried not to marvel at how peaceful he looked sleeping in her bed.

Once he was settled, she headed back to the kitchen, roughly waking Tam enough to get him to stumble to his own bed, and curled up on the couch.

Leah wasn't sure what the hells had happened between the two men that night, but the fact that they'd been walking together, arm in arm, and no one was bloodied or broken was a damn miracle.

She wondered how much of that they'd remember in the morning.

Chapter 9

"**G**ood morning!" The sing-song voice was annoyingly chipper and grating as Ash rolled away from the sound and tried to burrow under the pillow.

"Time to wake up, sleepy head!" That damned cheerful voice was far too loud.

Ash grabbed the blanket and pulled it over his head, hoping to smother the sound and disappear back into the peaceful darkness that had cocooned him just moments before.

"Go away," he groaned. His voice sounded pitiful and raw. His throat burned. Gods, what the hells had he done last night? Ash's head was pounding even as his stomach grumbled.

"Come on, soldier boy. I've got fresh cinnamon rolls and coffee in the kitchen. It will help, I promise."

Soldier boy. Shit. He'd assumed he was back in the inn, being harassed by the overly friendly innkeeper. Gods, he was out of it. He hadn't even recognized Leah's voice.

Ash took a deep, steadying breath, only to be overwhelmed by the scent of yeast, cinnamon, and something alluring but he couldn't think of its name. Squinting, he slowly opened his eyes and looked around.

Double shit. He was in her room. In her *bed.*

Ever-so-slowly, he sat up, facing the annoyingly cheerful half-fae assassin. She was beaming at him from her seat beside him on the bed. Her hair was loose and everywhere. Ash fought the sudden impulse to run his fingers through her soft, rose-gold locks. His eyes drifted down of their own accord, taking in her outfit. Or lack thereof. She was wearing an apron, but it didn't look as though she was wearing anything underneath.

Gods, take him. Had they slept together last night?

Blinking rapidly, Ash tried to force his memory to replay the last few hours, trying to recall exactly what he'd done the night before.

"Shit, are you gonna throw up again?" Leah leaned back a little, watching him intently. "You've gone really pale."

"I... did we... I mean, did I..." He couldn't get the words out. Ash's gaze flicked quickly from her nearly exposed chest to her eyes. An angry flush heated his skin as he watched her catch on to what he'd been failing to say.

"What? Oh, gods no!"

Ouch. But all right. That's what he wanted to hear anyway, wasn't it?

"You threw up on me last night. Well, a little. But I couldn't very well sleep in vomited clothes, so I didn't." The casual implication of her words—the fact that she'd slept naked—caused a different heat to flood his body, considerably lower.

Closing his eyes, Ash took another deep breath which turned out to be a terrible idea. The scent of her was everywhere, filling his senses and drowning out any rational thoughts.

Ash felt her shift from the bed, instantly missing the warmth of her presence.

"I actually came in here to get some fresh clothes. You can either stick around for the show," she tossed a wink over her shoulder and turned to her wardrobe, "or get out and let me dress in peace."

Ash was frozen in place. The apron covered her front completely, although it left little to the imagination. The back, however, left her plump, delicious ass entirely on display. Ash felt the sudden urge to pull her close and take a bite.

What the hells was wrong with him?

Leah knew she probably shouldn't have woken him up until after she'd gotten dressed, but she'd had one too many dreams about him—feeling the weight of him on top of her in a *very* different situation—that she'd decided fuck it. The man had nearly ruined her favorite boots. He could kiss her ass.

And maybe he would.

Leah chuckled to herself, hearing his breath catch when he saw how exposed she really was. She took her time picking out a pair of leggings and a long, sleeveless, green tunic. It was her favorite top. The gold embroidery along the hems was pure art. Annalise was a genius with a needle. She couldn't help herself as she put on a bit of a show, slipping on a pair of underwear and shimmying into the leggings before dropping the apron and pulling the tunic over her head. By the sound of it, Ash held his breath the entire time.

Smiling broadly, she turned back to face him. "Come on then, soldier boy. We've got work to do today. I hope you two worked through your bullshit because we'll be leaving for the capital today.

The king will be dead by tomorrow night. Then you'll never have to see us again." She turned to leave, but not before adding, "Unless you'd like to see more." With a sly grin, she sashayed out of the room, beaming internally when she heard the last of his breath whoosh out of his gaping mouth.

Gods, that was fun.

Tameer was waiting for her in the kitchen, a steaming cup of coffee in hand as he lounged at the table, eyes closed to block out the sunlight.

"Did you boys have fun last night?" she teased.

"Gods, that man. No human should have a tolerance that high. I've never failed to drink some fool under the table until last night."

"Was that the goal? Get him drunk and learn all his secrets?" Leah poured herself some coffee and grabbed a muffin from the baked sheet. Walking to join her friend at the table, she wondered just how much Ash had revealed to Tameer. Maybe getting stupidly drunk had actually been good for them.

Tameer took a swig of his coffee, sitting upright and squinting his eyes. "That wasn't the original plan, no. The original plan was to slit his throat and be done with it."

Leah glared at him. "You can't be serious. You thought you could get him drunk and kill him? What the hells, Tam?" He was insane and idiotic. Did he truly think he could get the drop on a *captain* of the King's Guard? It was a wonder Tam hadn't gotten himself killed years ago.

"That *was* the plan. Until he started talking." Tameer paused, seeming to remember the details of the night before, if a little slowly. "I get it now." His voice was soft, a hint of emotion marring his words.

"He told you, then? About his reasons for wanting the king dead?" Leah was relieved. If Tam knew the truth, then he'd understand her motives and they could finally get on the same page.

"About his mom? Yeah. Fuck, man. That's some heavy shit. I'm surprised he made it this far without getting himself killed trying to end that piece of shit."

Nodding her agreement, Leah opened her mouth to speak but was interrupted by the sound of shuffling feet making their way down the hall and into the kitchen. Sharing a quick *we'll talk later* look with Tam, she rose and poured a cup of coffee for Ash.

"Cream? Sugar? Milk?" She addressed the severely hungover guard with a cheery smile. She wasn't normally this perky in the morning, but seeing their misery had lit a fire of joy in her. Something about seeing them pay the price for dumb choices just brightened her morning.

"Black, please." Ash made his way slowly to the table, landing hard on her recently vacated chair, and took a long pull from her mug.

"Excuse me, soldier boy, that was *my* coffee." Leah replaced her half-drained mug with the fresh one she'd poured for him and went back for a refill.

"Shit. Sorry. What did you put in there, anyway? It's so thick with sugar it's practically syrup." Ash made a face as he took the correct mug and drained it in three gulps.

"Rude. Some of us like to savor our morning caffeine. And there is a normal amount of sugar in my cup. Plus a dash of cinnamon and nutmeg." Leah laughed as Ash made a face of pure disgust. "I like my coffee with a little extra oomph. You just don't know what good is, that's all."

Ash looked prepared to argue further, but Tameer spoke up, effectively ending their petty disagreement. "When do we leave? Is your potion all cured and shit?"

Leah stuck her tongue out at Ash, letting him know he hadn't won, they were just calling a temporary ceasefire. "The potion, as you so inaccurately call it, is a combination of nightshade, belladonna, and white willow. It's a poison, not some damn pixie magic in a bottle."

Tameer gave her a teasing smile. Gods, she hated when he implied her talents were magic. He knew it too, the ass.

"It should be ready. Last night was the full moon. The nightshade should be fully charged and the poison will be at its most potent in about thirteen hours. It doesn't leave us a lot of time for mistakes, but I've never needed much time for such things." Leah liked to brag, but the truth was, this was going to be the tightest schedule she'd ever had on an assassination. And it was the highest-stakes assassination she'd ever attempted.

All to protect her adopted sister and unborn nibling.

"We need to get moving then," Ash announced, rising to his feet with a sudden urgency.

The world tilted on its axis and Ash nearly fell face-first onto the rough tile floor. He threw a steadying hand out and grabbed hold of something soft and warm. It didn't stop his free-fall, but the softness cushioned the blow. Ash was grateful for whatever had kept him from cracking his head on the floor until he heard the cushion grunt.

"What the fuck?" Tameer exclaimed.

Ash heard the shuffling of furniture and feet, then someone attempted to shift his weight off the soft warm thing that had kept his hungover ass from causing himself serious injury.

"Gods, you really can't hold your liquor, can you?" Leah groaned as she shoved his chest. She either wasn't trying that hard to get him off of her or—more likely—she didn't have the brute strength it would take to move him.

Ash blinked, taking an embarrassingly long time to process what had just happened. He'd lost his balance and grabbed her? She'd been on the other side of the room... Had she rushed to his aide? That seemed unlikely. She liked to tease him, but Ash was fairly certain she didn't actually *like* him at all. She was merely tolerating him as a means to an end. Right?

Ash propped himself up on his elbows, his body lay flat atop hers as he looked down, studying her face and trying to understand her actions.

Leah watched him closely, a hint of heat in her eyes as she flicked her focus from his gaze to his lips and back again. She absentmindedly rolled her bottom lip between her teeth and Ash was suddenly very aware of all the places their bodies touched. His legs were firmly settled between hers, almost cradling him in their warmth.

"Would you two like the room?" There was humor in Tameer's voice as he sat back in his chair, clearly accepting that his friend wasn't in any danger or seriously injured.

Ash mentally shook himself and pushed off from the ground slowly.

"Are you ok?" Leah asked, standing and placing a gentle hand on his chest. "Your eyes rolled back in your head and you looked a little possessed."

"How does one become 'a little possessed'? Isn't that an all-or-nothing kind of thing?" Tameer rose and offered Ash his arm, helping him back to his chair while Ash tried to process what the hells just happened.

"If you're possessed by something weak, or you have incredible mental strength, I think that would count as a little possessed." Leah and Tameer continued to debate quite possibly the stupidest argument Ash had ever heard, but he tuned them out. Taking several deep breaths, he tried to will his body to get over this hangover quickly. They had work to do and they really needed to get to it. The longer the king lived, the more people would die. He was a tyrant of the first order and needed to be stopped.

Leah's face came into view. "You're all right, soldier boy." She placed a fresh mug in front of him. Not coffee. Something herbal and sweet smelling. "Drink this. It's my fool-proof hangover cure. Have you back to jumping out of chairs without falling on unsuspecting ladies in no time."

Ash thought he heard Tameer mutter something like, "You're no lady," but he couldn't be sure. He accepted the mug with a grateful nod and took a tentative sip. It was delicious, whatever it was. Ash marveled at his own behavior: willingly accepting and drinking gods only knew in the home of a half-fae assassin without even stopping to question it. A week ago, he would have killed Leah on sight. Now, he was sleeping in her bed, admiring her ass, and wondering what it would feel like to be cradled between her legs without clothes to separate them.

Gods, take him. He was falling for her magic and charms. And he didn't even mind.

Chapter 10

Leah watched Ash closely for the next few hours. He'd inhaled her tonic and was looking remarkably better, but it wasn't exactly the miracle cure she'd implied. If he collapsed again, she wanted to make sure he didn't smack his head. She had a plan to kill the king, but it required the beast of a man. If he couldn't stay upright, she'd need a new plan.

Which was fine. She could just go back to her original plan. So why did she keep watching him? Worrying about him? Sticking close to him as they moved around her house, packing and setting the alarms and traps so no one could break in while they were gone. Why was she so worried about this man who'd only come here to kill her?

She'd tried to convince herself it was just about the job, but that logic had failed her when he'd been lying on top of her. It had taken all of her self-control not to wiggle under him just to get a rise out of him. Or to lean up and bite his lip instead of her own.

Gods, she was so screwed.

Only an idiot would fall for the man who'd been sent to kill her. And she was *not* an idiot. Just a sucker for a pretty face. That's all this was, she told herself over and over. She just needed to get laid.

Leah's eyes tracked his movements around her kitchen, collecting their dishes from breakfast and wiping down the table. She couldn't stop her mind from wandering. Vivid images of him laying her back on that table. Tangling his fingers in her hair that he'd found so offensive. Feeling his body pressed against hers, flushed skin on skin. The length of him poised at her entrance... teasing her...

"Hey, you're looking a little distracted there," Tameer stepped pointedly into her view.

Leah blinked, shaking her head to try and rid herself of those images. Heat flushed her skin as she chewed her lip.

"Want some ice water? Your skin is all red and flushed," Tameer teased. "You getting a fever? Maybe you need to go lay down. Take care of yourself, if you catch my meaning."

Leah attempted to glare at him, but it mostly came out as a smirk. Damn him, he knew her too well.

"I'm fine, thank you very much." Leah turned from Tameer, realizing that Ash was staring at them with a look of confusion and curiosity. On second thought, Leah filled a glass with ice and water and drained it. Maybe Tam was right. A little cold water would help soothe her flushed nerves.

Ash watched her, a single eyebrow raised as a smirk tugged at his lips, but he didn't say a word. He knew what they'd been talking about. He might not have known the explicit images that had been playing in her mind, but Leah was starting to wonder if he'd object at all. The way his eyes had heated when he'd been on top of her, not to mention the fact that he'd clearly enjoyed the view when she'd been getting dressed earlier... He might be up for a quick romp. Something to clear their heads and release some tension.

"Tam," she spoke without taking her eyes off the soldier suddenly crowding her mental space. "I need you to go into town. Get some travel food. Dried meat, cheeses, etc. You know what to get." She broke eye contact with Ash then, turning her full focus on Tameer. "Take your time."

Tameer chuckled but nodded. Without another word, he turned on his heel and disappeared out the door.

The silence in the house was oppressive as Leah and Ash stared at each other from across the small dining room.

"Listen," Leah finally said. "I know you don't like me, but-"

"I never said I don't like you," Ash interrupted. "I don't trust you. Well, I didn't trust you."

"But you do now?" That was news to her.

"I must. I've been eating your food, drinking your drink, and passing out drunk in your bed. Those aren't exactly the actions of a distrustful person, are they?"

Leah hadn't really thought about it like that, but it was obvious when he laid it out like that. He had been very trusting, which should have been noteworthy if she hadn't been so fixated on her physical attraction to the man.

"So you don't hate me? You aren't secretly plotting my demise?" Leah teased, but there was a little too much truth in her fears. She liked him. She hated to admit it, but she really liked this soldier and she wanted him to like her too. Dammit.

Seeming to sense the weight of her words and the anxiety in her voice, Ash took a few slow steps towards her, hands up in surrender. "I don't want to kill you. Not anymore, anyway. I know I didn't make the best first impression. I came in with a lot of bigoted thoughts about your people—fae and criminals—but I can admit when I'm wrong." He was very close to her now. Not crowding her, but definitely in her space. If she wanted to get away, though, she could. Instead, she took a step toward him, taking his hands and placing them on her waist. His breath caught at the contact, but he didn't pull away.

Words failed her as Leah tried to think of how to broach the subject of a fling. She was no stranger to one-night stands, and while this was technically morning, she was hopeful that he'd be amenable to the idea. However, it felt crass and heartless to ask such a thing in the bright daylight. Instead, she let her body do the talking.

Pressing up on the tips of her toes, she held his gaze as her lips hovered just out of reach of his. Giving him the option to step back and put an end to this right here and now.

To her great relief, he closed the distance. His lips were surprisingly soft and tentative. Like he couldn't quite believe this was happening. She couldn't believe it either. She'd never kissed someone who planned to kill her before. It was exhilarating. Although, maybe this feeling had more to do with the man she was now firmly pressed against, and less to do with how they met.

His hesitation only lasted a breath. His fingers dug into where she'd placed them on her hips, pulling her closer still. Leah wrapped her arms around his neck, dragging him down to meet her as she placed her feet firmly on the ground. When his tongue sought entry into her mouth, she willingly and enthusiastically consented. The taste of him was unlike anything she'd ever experienced. It was tangy and sweet—likely a result of her tonic—and intoxicating. She was utterly engulfed by him and regretted nothing.

Ash held this woman—this murderous fae—in his arms and felt like he'd finally found where he belonged. His life had always been fraught with violence and despair, but standing in this assassin's kitchen, tasting her and feeling the warmth of her body flush against his own... he could only think to describe it as heavenly.

He wasn't sure how long they stood like that, learning the feel of each other, but when their kiss finally broke he was out of breath and more than willing to dive right back in.

"This really isn't sanitary," Leah teased, toying with the hair at the base of his neck and biting her lip.

Ash looked around, realizing they hadn't stayed in one spot, as he'd imagined. He had her backed against the table, practically sitting on the cinnamon rolls she'd baked for them that morning.

He placed a chaste kiss on her lips and moved to take a step back.

"Where do you think you're going?" She fisted his shirt and pulled him right back, hoisting herself onto the table and wrapping her legs around his waist.

Ash's body reacted immediately, ready and willing to take her here and now. Still, he held back. Taking a few steadying breaths, he tried to regain control of his body. "I thought, maybe you didn't want to... I mean, we don't really know each other. This probably isn't a good idea."

Leah nodded, although her legs tightened around him, pulling him closer and pressing him against her. "That's true. But I don't actually give a fuck. If it's all right with you, I'd like to have a little fun before we go off on a potential suicide mission."

Well, when you put it like that... he thought and quickly recaptured her mouth with his.

Scooping her up, much the same way he'd watched Tameer carry her out of the tavern that first night, Ash stumbled down the hall to her bedroom. They'd blow off some steam, get better acquainted, and then head off to kill the king. And probably get themselves killed in the process.

Chapter 11

Leah lay half on top of her would-be killer, her skin still warm from their activities. Ash had been so much more than she'd expected—in more ways than one. He was drifting to sleep as they lay together, legs intertwined, his hand tracing lazy circles on her hip.

"That was... unexpected," he said, placing a gentle kiss on her head. "Amazingly unexpected."

Leah shifted, resting her chin on his chest as she studied his expression, looking for hints of regret or discomfort at what they'd just done. To her surprise, he was smiling. Pure joy and happiness she hadn't thought he'd even been capable of, beamed back at her as he held her gaze.

She'd been fooling herself if she thought she could fuck this man and just move on with her life. Somehow, between trying to kill her and successfully bedding her, that damn man had wormed his way into her heart.

Shit.

Leah just finished tying her boots when Tameer came loudly into the house.

"I hope everyone is dressed and ready to go! We're killing daylight here, people!"

Gods, her best friend truly was obnoxious sometimes. Chuckling to herself, Leah grabbed her bag, flung it over her shoulder, and met him in the kitchen.

"Do you have to be *so* loud? The house isn't that big, Tam." She tossed her bag on the counter and began filling it with the travel biscuits she'd made the night before, as well as a waterskin.

"Just wanted to make sure I wasn't gonna walk in on anything. I've seen your ass enough to last me a lifetime." He ducked just in time to avoid getting hit in the face with the muffin that she threw at him. "Rude," he muttered, picking up the muffin and taking a dramatic bite.

"Yes, we had sex. Now grow up. He went to get his things from the inn. He'll meet us at the crossroads out of town, so quit bitching and let's go."

Leah threw her bag back over her shoulder, grabbed two muffins—one for herself and one for Ash—and they were out the door.

Time to kill the king.

Vexia wasn't far from Ravendale. Ash had made the trek in a matter of hours, but traveling with Leah and Tameer was slow. Painfully slow. They left Vexia in the late morning. They should have been walking into the city walls by mid-afternoon. Instead, they'd taken their sweet time, stopping to pick flowers, have snacks, sharpen weapons, and just drag this trip on for hours. Ash was wound tighter than a bowstring.

"What the hells is wrong with you both?" he finally snapped after their third stop in as many hours. "We should be there by now, but you two keep dragging your feet and making this trip take a thousand times longer than it reasonably should."

Tameer glared at him, but Leah smiled. "We aren't in a hurry, Ash. Rushing makes you sloppy."

"So does being an uptight, self-righteous ass," Tameer grumbled under his breath.

"I've been on military campaigns with hundreds of soldiers that move more efficiently than the two of you."

Leah rolled her eyes, then whispered something to Tameer. The man nodded and wandered off the path and into the woods that surrounded them. "Listen, I know you're used to doing things a certain way, and you're nervous about working with us, but I'm quite literally the best in the world at this. You have to relax and let me do this my way. Your way—charging in, blades at the ready—is just going to get us killed."

Ash resented her implications: namely that he didn't know what he was doing. He hated it even more because he knew she was right. He was a soldier, a guard. He'd never been on any stealth missions. That wasn't his skill set. He was an excellent leader and protector, but he knew he needed to defer to her judgment when it came to this sort of in-the-shadows mission. Assuming he wanted to live through the experience.

Watching her bite her lip, remembering how it felt to have those lips on his body... yeah, he definitely needed to live through this mission.

Leah reached a hand out toward him. Grudgingly, he took it, twining their fingers and placing an apologetic kiss on the back of her hand.

"I know you're anxious to get this over with, soldier boy." She beamed up at him. "But rushing in is dangerous. Plus, the best time to poison someone is when they're already drunk. There's a banquet tonight, celebrating the impending birth of Queen Irena's baby. King Odker will be drinking like a fish tonight. You just have to get me and Tameer in as servants for the night. I'll slip him a little something once he's too drunk to notice. You wait for him in his chambers. This will all work out fine, Ash."

She called him by his name, squeezing his hand. Ash loved the sound of his name on her lips. It sounded almost as sweet as when she was moaning it hours before.

Ash smiled at the memory, his gaze heating as he watched her pull that damn lip back between her teeth. She knew. She knew exactly where his thoughts had gone and she'd gone there with him. Ash leaned down, intending to bite that lip himself when Tameer shuffled back onto the path with them.

"Are we good? Did you get him to chill the fuck out?"

Gods, take him. Ash rolled his eyes, placed a kiss on Leah's head, and began walking down the path again, dragging her along with him.

The sky was quickly fading from pink to a deep lavender when they reached the castle gates. Leah had pulled her hair into a tight bun on the top of her head, throwing a dull brown wig on to cover the evidence of her fae parentage. Ash released her hand as they approached the gate, nodding to the guards and saying something to them. The guards looked at her and Tameer with a hint of suspicion but when Ash said something else, their gaze shifted from suspicion to pity. The guards waved the three of them through without another word.

Once they were out of earshot, Leah asked, "What did you say to them?"

"Yeah, they looked ready to arrest us for a second. Then it was like they thought we were being escorted to the executioner's block."

Ash grimaced over his shoulder, not bothering to slow down. "You're not too far off. I told them you were hired to serve the king tonight at the banquet. That's basically a death sentence."

Gods, this fucking king. He couldn't die fast enough. Leah wished she'd added a little something extra to the poison. Something a little more agonizing. Maybe something that would melt his insides.

It was too late now, but damn. King Odker really was the worst human on the planet. The country—hells, the world—would be better off once he was gone.

Chapter 12

Leah had been in the castle before, but never during something so lavish. The Great Hall was decorated with seasonal bouquets on each of the round tables that encircled the room. A massive dance floor had been left in the center of the room, with the king and queen seated at a long table on a raised dais across the room. Irena looked indescribably uncomfortable, although Leah couldn't tell if that was a result of her marriage to the murderous king or the corset she was clearly wearing far too tightly in her seventh month of pregnancy.

Leah and Tameer were dressed in the maroon and black garb of the banquet waitstaff. Tameer had a tray of hors d'oeuvres—snails in a garlic butter sauce with a toasted baguette—on the far side of the room. With Ash's glowing endorsement, Leah had been given the task of wine bearer for the king. He was meant to be her sole focus and his cup was never supposed to get below half. They'd been there for two hours now and it was a wonder the man was still upright.

Leah had taken to standing directly between the king and queen, enabling her to refill his goblet with ease while overhearing any and all conversations between the royals. Not to mention, Irena had visibly relaxed when she saw Leah enter the room with the king's serving decanter.

The king leaned over now, grabbing Irena's arm. From a distance, it might have looked affectionate, but from Leah's vantage point, she could see his fingers digging into her skin. It would leave a bruise.

"If thish chil ishn't a boy, I'll have yer head." He slurred his words, but the message was painfully clear. Irena's face paled, but she offered her husband a smile and nod. Attempting to keep up appearances and pacify the violent bastard in one simple action.

King Odker released her and took another long swig of his goblet.

Now. It had to be now. The man was going to pass out soon. She needed to dose him and get this shit over with. Irena didn't need the stress of this man and his threats hanging over her any longer.

Deftly, Leah slipped the poison vial from her sleeve, popped the cork, and poured it into the decanter. Slipping the now-empty vial back up her sleeve, she swirled the decanter a bit, mixing the poison in with the king's favorite wine, before refilling his goblet.

It was time to bring this reign of terror to an abrupt and justly violent end.

Ash was anxious. No. That was an understatement. Ash was freaking the fuck out. Well, as much as a highly trained captain of the King's Guard *can* freak out. He was pacing in the hall just outside the Great Hall. The exit the king would be using any minute now, after ingesting Leah's poison and suddenly needing a toilet.

Any minute now.

Gods, this was taking too long. He was going stir crazy just—

The king practically burst through the door, stumbling into the private hallway.

"Ash," he muttered, grabbing Ash by the collar. "Get me to my rooms. Now."

Throwing the king's arm over his shoulder, Ash took the brunt of the king's weight and practically carried the drunken asshole to his chambers. The second they made it into the room, Odker threw himself from Ash's shoulder and half ran, half fell into the bathroom, seeking relief.

The sound of his retching echoed throughout the empty chambers. Queen Irena had her own rooms. Their suites were connected by a door, but they were rarely alone together. Thank the gods for that. Irena would likely have been long dead if she'd been forced to share a room with the king.

Pulling his dagger, Ash began pacing again. This was his time. *This* was his chance. Leah had set him up perfectly. All he had to do was go in there and slice the monster's throat. End this all before anyone else was hurt. He'd finally get revenge for his mother and rid the world of that violent man's vile influence.

So why was he still here?

A quick knock on the door forced Ash to stop his pacing. It was the knock Leah told him she'd use when the path was clear and they could sneak out through the servants' quarters. He was supposed to have killed the king already, dammit.

Quickly, he opened the door and urged her in, checking the hall once more before closing and locking the door.

"What's wrong?" she whispered, hearing the king still retching and groaning in the bathroom.

"I don't know. I've never killed someone in cold blood like this. They've always had a fighting chance. This just feels... wrong somehow."

Leah took a deep breath like she was trying to contain her emotions before she spoke. "I understand your hesitance, but he's a killer. If we don't stop him, Irena and the baby will be next. Not to mention all the servants and citizens who have been suffering at that man's hands for decades. I can finish him off, if you don't think you can."

She pulled a wickedly sharp, curved dagger from her back. Ash was surprised. He hadn't even seen the sheath there, and he'd been watching her closely all day.

Blinking, he shook his head. "I need to do this. For my mother. For—"

The king came stumbling out of the bathroom, pale and sweating. His eyes were unfocused until they saw Leah. The thin veneer that kept his kingly appearance in the forefront snapped, revealing the monster beneath.

"I see you brought me a toy," he stumbled over his words and his feet as he crossed the room, grabbing hold of Leah before Ash could stop him. Leah struggled under the man's weight, dropping her blade as he took hold of her hair. He pulled, as though he planned to haul her to his bed by her scalp, only to come away with her wig. Leah's pink hair uncoiled, falling freely from its containment and flowing down her back like a beautiful pink waterfall.

King Odker stared, baffled, for a moment, then opened his mouth and cried out. "Guards!! Guards, the fae assassin is here!"

Ash leapt across the room, smothering the man's words with his hand and holding his dagger to the king's throat. Odker struggled until Ash pressed harder with the blade, a single drop of blood pooling at the tip of the steel. "Shut your fucking mouth," he growled into the king's ear.

Leah righted herself, trying to wrap her hair back up in the wig as quickly as possible.

There was a loud banging on the door, guards shouting through the thick wood, demanding the door be opened. In a heartbeat, Ash heard the sound of an axe hacking into the wood. The guards were going to break into the room. Sooner rather than later.

They needed to move.

Leah gave up on her hair, throwing the wig down, retrieving her lost dagger while unsheathing a second and adopting a defensive stance.

"Just slice his throat and let's get the fuck out of here," she said, never taking her eyes off the door.

Ash pivoted, putting the king between himself and the door. He positioned himself in front of Leah. The guards were through the door before Ash could take a second breath.

"Unhand him, traitor!" yelled the first guard. Ash recognized the man's face, but couldn't recall his name.

He took a step back, keeping his blade at the king's throat and guiding Leah toward the king's balcony. Below was the river. If they could just get to the balcony, they could jump into the water and swim to safety.

Leah seemed to understand his intent and began moving more quickly toward the open balcony doors.

"I said unhand him!" the guard shouted again as more soldiers flooded into the room and moved to encircle them.

"I can't do that. This man is a monster. You all know it. He can't be allowed to live another day. The world will be better off without him." Ash pressed the blade harder. The king grunted and the soldiers froze.

"Ash," came a familiar voice. Stevenson. One of the guards who'd come to his home all those years ago, killed his mother, and left him for dead. "Don't be an idiot. You kill him and we'll have to kill you."

"You already tried to kill me," Ash spat. "Twenty years ago. You came to my home, slaughtered my mother, and tried to do the same to me."

Ash waited for a look of recognition to cross Stevenson's face. When none came, Ash realized that he wasn't the only child the king had ordered murdered. Likely, Stevenson had killed so many of the king's bastards that he wouldn't remember Ash or his mother.

Rage flowed anew. A cry of unbridled anger tore from Ash's throat as he dragged his blade across the king's throat. The warmth of the man's blood now pouring from the gaping wound was jarring as the cool wind blew in from the balcony. Ash hadn't even realized he'd made it outside.

Leah grabbed his arm, trying to pull him with her over the side, just as the guards charged.

In a moment of clarity, Ash dropped the king, turned to face Leah, and pushed her over the balcony balustrade. He heard her cry out his name as the guards tackled him to the ground.

Ash strained to hear the splash that would signify she'd made it to safety as the guards hoisted him up, binding his hands behind his back and hauling him out of the king's chambers and down to the dungeons.

The sound of his assassin hitting the water was the last thing he heard before Stevenson strode up and knocked him out with the pommel of his sword.

Chapter 13

As Tameer hauled her out of the water, Leah struggled to get out of his hold and swim back across the river. She'd washed up on the wrong side, nearly a mile from the castle. It was a miracle Tam had found her, honestly, considering how far downstream she'd gone. They'd both snuck out of the party at the same time, with the intention of meeting at the crossroads when the job was done.

Then the job had gone sideways.

The last thing she'd seen before the icy, dark water swallowed her was Ash being tackled by four guards and dragged away.

The king was dead, but Ash was soon to follow.

Leah fought to get free of Tameer. "I have to go back! They took him. The guards have him. We have to save him!"

Tameer refused to release her. Instead, he pulled her in tighter, wrapping her in his arms as sobs wracked her body. He wasn't supposed to get captured. Her plan was flawless. If the damned man hadn't let his conscience get in the way, he'd be the one embracing her right now.

"He's gone, Leah. You can't save him. He knew this was a deadly mission. We all did. We knew if any of us got captured, it would mean death. If you go back for him now, you'll only get yourself killed too."

Leah refused to acknowledge his words, even if they were the exact same sentiments she'd expressed before they'd ventured into the castle walls. It had been a suicide mission. She'd been a fool to think they'd all walk away.

"He saved me," she said, her voice raw and cracked. "He pushed me over the balcony and let the guards take him." She sat back, locking eyes with Tameer. "Why? Why would he do such a stupid thing?" Tears were flowing freely now.

Tameer pulled her into him, wrapping his arms around her and pressing a kiss to her forehead. "He wanted to keep you safe. I can understand that impulse."

Leah lost track of time as she cried herself into exhaustion. They must have drifted off at some point because Leah woke with a start to the sound of a cardinal singing his morning tune.

Tameer still held her, but they'd shifted to a horizontal position. To any passersby, they would have looked like two lovers enjoying a night under the stars. In reality, Leah felt as though her heart had been ripped from her chest. She was in agony and utterly numb at the same time. She laid there for a while longer, watching the sun slowly brighten the sky.

Tameer tightened his grip around her, "We should go. It's not safe here right now. The king is dead. They think they caught the killer, but the guards saw you too. They'll have search parties looking all over for the pink-haired fae who helped kill their king. It's going to be chaotic for a while."

Leah didn't want to leave Ash. She couldn't go if she thought she could save him.

Tameer took her chin in his hand, gently pulling her gaze from the castle walls to lock with his. "You can't stay here. Your hair alone will make you a target. Not to mention, you're a wanted assassin. You have to get out of here. Go home. I'll get back inside and see what I can do. I've still got connections with the Guild. Maybe we can spring him before it's too late."

Leah's brain was fried. She knew that, rationally, she couldn't be the one to sneak around the castle. Not now, when they would be on high alert. Especially since she'd lost her wig and her rose gold hair was on full display. The idea of leaving Ash to his fate, and praying to the gods that Tameer still had reliable connections in the Thieves Guild, felt wrong. Like she was one step away from giving up.

Tameer knelt before her, taking her face firmly in his hands. "Leah, get up. Go. I will do what I can, but I can't take care of him if I'm worried about you." He grabbed her hands and pulled her to her feet. "Head back to Vexia. I'll see what I can do and be back as soon as possible."

The dungeon was dark. No, that wasn't accurate. The cell Ash had been put in was pitch black. There was no difference between his eyes being opened and closed. His hands were still bound behind his back, but he'd managed to get himself into a seated position against the wall.

He'd done what he came here to do. The king was dead. His mother had been avenged. He could rest easy now. So why was his heart still racing? Why was he still so anxious?

Leah. He hoped she'd made it out all right. He'd heard her splash, but he couldn't be sure it had been the sound of her reaching safety. The balcony had been several stories above the ground, and he couldn't be sure Leah had landed in the middle of the river. She could have just as easily landed too close to the banks. Broken her legs. Or worse: her neck. She could be laying dead on the riverside and he'd never know.

Ash was trapped in a prison cell, awaiting certain death, and all he could think about was the safety and well-being of a half-fae assassin. Gods, he was a love-sick fool.

It was love, he'd determined, that caused him such anguish. He'd fallen in love with the girl he'd fully intended to kill. Ash smiled ruefully to himself. He was a fool, all right. But he had only one regret: that he didn't get a chance to tell her how he felt before he died.

His death was imminent, that was undeniable. He'd killed the king, in front of witnesses. Hells, the witnesses were fuck-ing *King's Guards*. He wouldn't be walking away from this one. It had been worth it, but he couldn't shake the little part of him that wished he'd been able to tell Leah he loved her. Kiss her one last time.

Maybe in the next life.

Ash had no way of knowing how much time had passed when he heard the door swing open. The light from the torches in the hall temporarily blinded him. Turning away, Ash tried his best to shield his eyes. Someone shuffled into the room with a small lantern, closing the door behind them.

"Can you stand?" It was a woman's voice. That was unexpected. Ash didn't think the king employed any female soldiers or guards.

When he looked up, Ash thought for a moment that he'd truly lost his mind. The woman before him wasn't a guard or soldier. It was the queen.

"Majesty." He made to bow, but barely made it to a kneeling position before Queen Irena set her lantern down and rushed to his side.

"Please, there's no need for that. You are here because of me." Even in the faint light, Ash could see tears dancing along her eyelashes.

"Your Highness, you haven't done anything to me." Ash shifted from his knees to standing before her, keeping his head bowed. "I would like to say I killed the king to protect you, but if I'm being honest, I killed him for selfish reasons. He killed my mother and left me for dead."

Queen Irena blinked, silently processing his words and their implication. "Are you one of his children?" she asked softly.

Ash nodded. He couldn't bring himself to vocalize his relationship with the monster of a man. He rarely wanted to acknowledge that the king's blood ran through his veins, but it was undeniable. At least the man was dead now and couldn't forcibly impregnate any more women, or kill or abandon any more children.

The queen looked as though she wanted to say more, but stopped herself. She moved behind him and freed his hands from the bindings. "We need to hurry. The guards will be back soon. Tameer is waiting."

Tameer? Where was Leah? He was about to ask when Queen Irena picked up her lantern again and cracked the door open. She motioned for him to follow her and they slipped out of the oppressive cell and off to freedom.

They crept down the hall in near silence, the only sound that of the Queen's skirts dragging along the rough stone floor.

Tameer was, in fact, waiting at the end of a long hall of cells, before a tapestry depicting the God of Death on a throne of skulls. Tameer greeted Queen Irena with a warm—if brief—embrace, then nodded to Ash and pulled back the tapestry to reveal a tunnel. He motioned for them both to follow him.

The tunnel seemed to be slowly leading them upward. Ash wanted to ask about Leah, but he wasn't sure he had a right to ask after the woman he'd nearly gotten killed.

Queen Irena's breath was beginning to sound a bit labored when Tameer halted and motioned for them to stay put as he disappeared around a corner Ash hadn't seen in the dark tunnel.

"Are you all right, Your Majesty? Would you like to sit down?" Ash hated the idea of the queen creeping through dark, potentially dangerous tunnels to help him. Especially when she was with child. This sort of activity couldn't possibly be healthy for the baby.

Queen Irena waved him off. "I'm fine. I just need to catch my breath. This baby keeps kicking my lungs. It makes deep breaths challenging." She handed him the lantern and leaned back against the wall. Ash watched her nervously, but he wasn't in a position to question the queen.

Tameer reappeared, eyeing Queen Irena cautiously. "You good, Irena?"

Ash hated how casually Tameer addressed the queen. He got the impression that there was some history there, although he couldn't fathom how that could be.

Queen Irena raised a single eyebrow in condemnation. "The next person who questions my well-being will spend the next week in my dungeons. Are we clear?"

Tameer grinned widely. "Whatever you say, Your Majesty." He held out a hand but Queen Irena slapped it away, pushing off from the wall and stalking toward the end of the tunnel. Tameer shared a look with Ash, shrugged, and followed after the queen with Ash on his heels.

A small door waited at the end of the tunnel. Tameer jumped ahead of the queen, opening the door and sticking his head out before shoving it open and stepping out into the night. Queen Irena turned back to Ash and took his hands.

"Thank you, Captain. You saved my life and the life of my child. I'm sorry that I can't pardon you yet. Hopefully, I'll be able to get this whole shit show under control quickly. I'll pardon you as soon as I can." There were tears in her eyes again. Ash squeezed her hands, not trusting his voice to speak. "Go to Leah. Give her my thanks and my love."

Ash nodded and bowed as she released his hands. Turning to Tameer, she gave him a tight hug, kissing both of his cheeks and thanking him for his help.

"Let us know when the little one is born. We can't wait to meet our little nibling." Tameer placed a loving hand on the queen's prominent belly.

The confusion must have been written on Ash's face when Tameer turned to him. "What's got you twisted, pretty boy? The fact that an assassin and a thief might have a close bond with a queen?"

"What the hells is a nibling?" Ash blurted it out, not thinking about his vulgar language in front of the queen. Had Tam just made up that word on the spot to confuse him? There's no way that's a real word.

"Oh, that? Tameer chuckled. "It just means niece or nephew, but since we don't know the sex of the little human in there, we're sticking with gender-neutral terms for now." He turned back to Queen Irena. "Be safe. And seriously, the *second* that little person makes their entrance, we expect a raven to be pecking away at our window to announce the birth. We'll come rushing back to shower you with gifts."

"Of course," the queen said, beaming with love. "I'll send a message the instant this little terror makes their arrival. Now, go. Leah will never let me hear the end of it if you don't get back soon."

Ash stepped through the doorway and said one last grateful goodbye to the queen. She slipped away, disappearing with her lantern into the tunnel. Tameer closed the door that looked more like a weathered stone once closed, and turned to Ash.

"Ready to go home? Our girl is waiting and she's *very* impatient."

Home. Yes. Ash desperately wanted to go home to Leah.

Chapter 14

Two days. The king had been dead for two days. Ash had been taken to the dungeons two days ago. Tameer had promised to do whatever he could to free him two days ago.

Leah had been in the darkest pits of hells for two fucking days. She was going insane. She'd stress-baked enough muffins, cupcakes, cookies, and bread to feed the entire country for a month.

As she pulled the four hundredth tray of snickerdoodle cookies from the oven, she heard a sound outside.

Leah's heart skipped a beat as she held her breath; frozen in place as she strained to hear the sound again.

Voices. Male voices. Two distinct voices she'd recognize anywhere. One of which she'd feared she'd never hear again.

Leah threw the tray on the stovetop, rushing toward the door and throwing it open. Just beyond the curve in the path leading up to her house, she heard the crunch of their boots on the gravel and the gentle timber of their voices.

Leah ran as fast as her legs could carry her, tears streaming down her face as she laughed with joy and relief.

Ash saw her coming and immediately dropped the food he'd been chewing and raced to meet her halfway, scooping her into his arms and wrapping her in the tightest embrace she'd ever experienced.

"I was so worried," she said through her tears. "I saw them take you away and I thought..." Her voice failed her as he set her back on the ground, taking her face in his warm hands and placing gentle kisses on her forehead, cheeks, nose, and finally her lips. He smothered her fears with his soft but firm kisses. Banishing all of her worries and making her feel as light as a feather.

Tameer made a loud, coughing sound, as though he was dramatically trying to clear his throat. "I'm fine too, thanks for asking."

Leah disconnected from their kiss, turning to face Tameer although she stayed firmly in Ash's grasp. "I'm glad. I'm glad you're ok and I'm so fucking grateful that you were able to save him and both come back to me unharmed."

"Wait, who said he saved me? I could have saved myself, you know. I was the captain of the King's Guard. I'm quite adept at combat." Ash pulled her tighter to him, her back pressed snuggly against his unyielding chest.

She tilted her head back, practically looking straight up to see him. She glowed with a warmth and joy that was infectious. "Of course you could have, soldier boy. We all know you're very brave and strong."

Leah and Tameer laughed. Teasing him was quickly becoming their favorite way to pass the time, it seemed.

"I'll show you just how strong I am," Ash threatened. He turned Leah around and hauled her over his shoulder, giving her plump ass a quick swat as she squealed with a mixture of surprise and delight.

"Tameer," Ash said as he began striding toward the front door. "We're going to need some privacy. Why don't you go get a drink or seven?"

Leah could hear Tameer laughing as Ash hoisted her higher on his shoulder and strode purposefully into the house. He kicked the door closed and didn't slow down until he reached her bed. Tossing her onto the mattress, he deftly removed his tunic and turned his heated gaze on her.

Gods, take her.

She was never letting him out of her sight again.

Also by Mallory Wanless

The *turmio* trilogy:
Storm and Flame: Enchanted I
Blood and Destiny: Enchanted II
Reign and Ruin: Enchanted III

Enchanted Standalones:
Reclaiming the Frost: Enchanted IV

Vexia Standalone Novellas:
Of Poison and Passion

Coming soon:
Enchanted V
Enchanted VI

About the Author

Mallory lives in Texas with her husband and their two young boys. She spends her days homeschooling and full-time parenting. Her nights, and any free time she manages to carve out during the day, are devoted to reading and writing.

If you enjoy this story, please be sure to leave a review on your favorite sites. Thank you so much!

www.ingramcontent.com/pod-product-compliance
Lightning Source LLC
Chambersburg PA
CBHW040911010826
48978CB00013BB/1242